A Rose So Red

ARLA JONES

Contents

CHAPTER ONE

Rose And Arthur

Aislinn and Ian Manchester named their first baby girl Rose. Her lips reminded Aislinn of the pink rose petals in her rose garden, her eyes were beautiful azure blue like the summer sky, and her manners as the first child born in the duke's estate were perfect: she was quiet, easily pleased, and a happy child. She hardly ever cried. They loved their baby girl to the moon and back.

Ian Manchester had taken Arthur Smith with them to his estate. Arthur had helped save Aislinn and her father from Tower prison; thus, they all owed him their happiness and lives.

When Arthur saw Rose for the first time, he felt the earth tilt, as the baby's gaze was so intense. He knew this was the girl he would marry.

He did not know how he knew it, but he was sure of it. Arthur wasn't even sure how old he was. He guessed he was around eight years old but could be younger or older. No one had told him when he was born or who his parents were. He had lived on the streets for as long as he could remember. He was lucky When he met Manchester's family.

Rose was everything to Arthur, too. She was the cable tying him to this estate and the family, the center of his universe from the moment she was born.

The duke believed Arthur needed proper schooling and thus allowed him to study together with Rose. He was good at math and reading, but Rose was always better, although she never bragged or teased him if he answered wrong.

When they grew up, Rose was sent to a boarding school to learn the manners of a society girl, whereas Arthur stayed at the estate and took care of the garden. Gardening and especially roses were his favorites. He learned everything from the old gardener and then continued experimenting by himself. He learned how to improve the soil to get bigger flowers, how to prune the plants and take care of the bugs that would bite the leaves and flowers. He loved to create new rose varieties because every new rose reminded him of the duke's daughter.

Visitors adored walking around the estate's garden, and they often praised how beautiful the garden was.

On her sixteenth birthday, Rose came back to visit. She was even more beautiful than Arthur remembered. He stood by the driveway as her carriages stopped in front of the mansion. The servant hurried to open the door and helped her to climb down. She wore a light pink summer dress with a high waist and short sleeves revealing her bare arms. Her hair had darkened to a golden-brown color and was tied in a bun on her neck.

Arthur felt as if his heart had stopped for a second when Rose turned her blue eyes on him and smiled. He stood there like a fool and could not utter a word to greet her. Luckily, the duke and duchess rushed to hug their daughter, and the lady of the house exclaimed, "Rose, you look so beautiful. I bet there is no other girl as stunning as you at school. And you've grown. You look like a lady!"

Rose twirled around. "How do you like my new dress? It's the latest fashion from France. One of the girls at the boarding school took me to her dressmaker, and we got similar dresses."

Aislinn smiled. "You look gorgeous, darling. Let's go inside, and you can tell me all about your school." She put her arm around her waist, and they ambled inside.

Ian, Duke of Manchester, saw Arthur staring at Rose and strolled toward him. "Our baby is no longer a little girl. She's grown to be a lady."

Arthur looked dazed but managed to reply, "Yes, she has. She is the most beautiful Rose." He stood there like lightning had struck him, unmoving and staring at where Rose had been long after she had gone.

Ian gave her a quizzical look. He noticed Arthur's look. *He is lovestruck. The poor boy is infatuated with our daughter.*

Ian shook his head, patted Arthur on the back, and ordered, "Get back to work in the garden, Arthur."

His love is hopeless. A poor boy could never marry a duke's daughter. Never in this world. And never my daughter! She deserves a nobleman. It is time for her to be a debutante in London!

CHAPTER TWO

Rose and Lillian

The duke's whole household adored Rose. She had always been kind to everyone. She was a quick learner; thus, she was sent to a boarding school to learn new languages, dances, and etiquette and make new friends in the town. She was well-liked there, too, among her peers.

Lillian, Aislinn's maid, checked out Rose's new dresses she had ordered while at school. "I can copy the pattern and make more of these for you, Miss Rose," Lillian assured her. "We need to get light pink or blue material, and I'll sew them and make beautiful embroideries around the neckline and hem with beads and pearls. They would be perfect for the summer season in London."

"That would be wonderful," Rose replied and hugged the trusted maid. She held her for a moment and then asked, "You have not told me yet; how is your beau? I know you have been seeing that pastor in the village."

Lillian blushed. "Oh, miss. He is nice. We have walked in the garden together, and he reads me verses from the bible."

Lillian poked her with her elbow. "Is he going to ask you to marry him?"

Lillian wrung her hands. "I don't know. I would like that very much if he would. He is kind, and he would make a good husband."

"That is sweet, but do you love him?" Rose waggled her eyebrows.

Lillian sighed. "Yes, Charles Hemming has captured my heart." She pressed her hand over her chest.

Rose hugged her again. "That is wonderful. Maybe we will see a summer wedding!"

"We'll see. He has not asked me yet," Lillian muttered and turned her face to Rose. "How about you, miss Rose? Do you have anyone special?"

Rose laughed, and her laughter was always a kind, warm-hearted laughter. "No, I have not met anyone who would have made my heart twitterpated. "

Lillian patted her arm gently. "You will someday. It might happen this summer or next. You never know when the one you love will walk into your life, or perhaps you have already met the right one, but you have not paid attention to him. Sometimes, love comes later, not when you first meet someone."

Rose giggled. "You are so sweet, Lillian. I'm sure I will fall in love with the most wonderful man in the whole wide world! He will adore me in the dresses you make for me, and he won't be able to stop thinking about me. I will be the center of his world."

"That sounds so romantic," Aislinn said by the doorway as she walked inside. Both Lillian and Rose turned their heads to see her.

Rose said, "Mom, were you eavesdropping on us?"

Aislinn shook her head. "No, I didn't have to. Your laughter rang on the stairs. It was easy to hear you two talking." She adjusted her blue satin dress and sat down on a chair. "Have you finished with the dresses?"

Lillian nodded. "Yes, I can easily do more similar to the ones Miss Rose had on today. The pattern is really simple to make, but it does suit her well."

Aislinn nodded. "I agree. A high waist is good for all types of bodies. Perhaps, you can make one for me, too?" She turned her amethyst-colored eyes to Lillian, who eagerly nodded. "Yes, of course, Ma'am."

Aislinn got up. "Thank you, Lillian." She faced Rose and said, "I came to fetch you to have tea or coffee with us. Your father is waiting for us downstairs."

"Let's go." Rose jumped up from the bed where she had been sitting and straightened her dress with her hands. She had her mother's amethyst eyes but her father's darker hair. Her slender figure was like her mother's, but her inner strength and fast wit were inherited from her father.

Rose followed her mother out the door while Lillian stayed behind, gathering her sewing materials. Aislinn walked graciously down the stairs and led her daughter through the glass doors outside, where a small table was set with coffee and teapots, white porcelain cups, scones, sandwiches, and muffins.

Ian, Duke of Manchester, glanced up when he heard their steps. "There you are. I was waiting for you." He quickly stood up, helped both ladies sit down, and then sat himself.

CHAPTER THREE

Duke's Plan

Ian, the Duke of Manchester, was pleased to see how her daughter had gained gracious manners at the boarding school, and she behaved like a real lady.

Ian recalled the first time he had laid his eyes on his future wife, Aislinn Ackley. She was funny, curious, and unaware of her mesmerizing eyes and fairy-like beauty. Her daughter, Rose, had the same qualities.

Ian had been married seventeen years to Aislinn. His hair was still dark, but it had a few silver highlights. He was also busy with his duties in the House of Lords and overseeing his mansions and tenants at Norfolk's seaside and in London.

Aislinn glanced at her husband curiously. She knew Ian had something in his mind as he stared at their daughter and barely sipped his coffee. Aislinn clinked her cup with her spoon on purpose to wake Ian up from his reveries. It worked.

Ian quickly gazed at his wife, straightening his shoulders and clearing his throat. He leaned closer to Rose and said, "Rose, I have something to tell you."

"Yes, father." Rose turned her amethyst eyes to him, put down her cup of tea, and placed her hands on her lap.

"I have decided that you should be a debutante this summer and be introduced to the ton. You have learned etiquette, dancing, the French language, math, embroidery, and some bookkeeping. You would make a fine wife." Ian stopped and stared at his daughter.

Rose was calm. She didn't jump up excited nor rush to hug him or argue against his decision but sat there and nodded. She always agreed with what her father said. Ian was pleased with how well she had been educated and brought up.

If Ian had known what was in Rose's mind, he would not have been so satisfied. Rose had a mind of her own and didn't want to prance around like a prize horse and be sold to the highest bidder. She wanted to be in love with her future husband like her parents had been. She had learned to be amicable and agree to whatever her father said but then find a way to do it according to her own will. Rose was not stupid or dull. She was sharp and could easily figure out how to avoid doing tasks she didn't want to do. So, now Rose sat and smiled sweetly, but in her mind, she was already strategizing how to avoid the marriage trap.

Aislinn put down her teacup. She leaned forward to pat her daughter's hand and exclaimed happily, "That is so wonderful! Think about all the lovely parties and masquerades we will attend to!" She turned to her daughter, and her smile was wide and sincere. "You will love this summer in London."

Rose nodded and smiled. "I'm sure I will."

If Ian had given it more thought, he might have found Rose's consent suspect because she didn't seem exuberantly happy nor argue against the duke's plan. Ian should have realized that she was pretending to agree and not planning to find a husband this summer.

Ian himself had been a notorious rake and had taken his time before getting married at the age of thirty.

Rose kept smiling. She sipped her tea while her mother patted about the dresses, the parties, and where they could stay in London. When she heard her mother mentioning the townhouse, she raised her head and asked, "Do you mean Lord Ackley and Lady Olivia's house where my cousin Andre lives?"

Aislinn nodded. "Yes, of course. I'm sure they will be eager to see us."

Ian interrupted. "You can stay in my London townhouse."

Aislinn replied, "Yes, of course, we'll stay there, but it will be nice to visit my father and Lady Olivia, too. I must write them about our plans. Lady Olivia will be thrilled to have another debutante to introduce to the ton. Please, excuse me." She got up and rushed inside, leaving Rose with her father.

Ian squinted, stared at Rose, and muttered, "She seems to be more excited than you are."

Rose quickly replied, "She knows what to expect. I don't." And she was right. Aislinn had been a debutante, and Lady Olivia had introduced her to the ton and taught her dancing and etiquette skills.

Ian winced as he remembered the horror of the balls where all the mothers of the debutants flocked around the available gents all evening, trying to introduce their daughters of the marrying age. The daughters were usually shy and giggling, and he hated to dance with someone who could not even converse with him. Aislinn had been different. She had been sensible, beautiful, and witty. He sighed and gazed at his daughter. Rose would do well. She was practical, beautiful, and had good brains.

Chapter Four

Rose and Arthur

When Ian, the Duke of Manchester, returned inside to prepare his speech for the next session in the House of Lords, Rose decided to take a walk in the garden.

What Rose didn't know about their discussion had secretly listened. Arthur had never been one to eavesdrop on other people's conversations, and he did not mean to do so today either; however, the duke had looked so determined and had requested the family to have a tea break with him, so Arthur had thought there was the reason for it. He had meandered near the terrace where the duke's family had sat and heard how Ian had announced his idea for Rose's summer. Arthur inhaled deeply when he heard the plan, and his hand squeezed the rake so hard his knuckles turned white. He didn't want Rose to go away to find a husband. He wanted Rose for himself. He had peered through the small gap between glass and door frame, only catching a brief glimpse of Rose sitting with her parents, but he could easily hear the duke's voice.

When the duchess and the duke had returned inside, and Rose was left alone, Arthur quickly proceeded to rake further away from the terrace, so she would not suspect him of eavesdropping.

He recalled the first time he had met the duke. Ian had been so serious. Aislinn and her father had been imprisoned in Tower, and Ian was looking for the real culprits who had tried to assassinate the queen. Luckily for Arthur, he had seen the Indian servants when they met in a bar near the docks. Arthur's help had been instrumental in getting Aislinn and her father, George Ackley, out of the Tower; thus, Ian had promised to take care of him.

As a child, Arthur had been too skinny but handsome. His hair had been reddish, but now it had turned to more mahogany than red. His eyes were green like the moss on the side of the tree in the forest. He had learned manners in the duke's household and was smart, too.

When Ian had left Rose, she ambled out the terrace door into the front lawn and looked up to the blue sky, wondering what to do next. She breathed in deeply, willing her emotions to calm down. Like many times before, she had wanted to argue, but she didn't want to upset anyone, especially not her father. Now, it was time to calmly think of a way to undo his marriage plan.

Her emotions continued to swirl inside, so she continued onward, her slippered feet carrying her further into the path leading to the rose garden, where she came upon a small white pavilion with smooth columns and seats on both sides. If you wanted to have a secret meeting with someone, that would be a great place for it as it was surrounded by lilac shrubs and climbing white and pink roses, making it impossible to see who was inside until you were by the doorway. She sat down on one of the benches and sighed.

Arthur had followed her, and when he saw Rose alone in the pavilion, he approached quietly. He knocked on one of the columns to let his presence known, and when Rose looked up and saw him, she smiled.

"Come and sit next to me, Arthur," she said, patting the bench next to her. She moved her wide light pink hem away so that Arthur would not sit on it.

"How are you, Rose?" Arthur asked, staring into her eyes. He saw sadness in them.

"My father wants me to find a husband this summer. I have to go to London and attend balls," she replied quietly. Her finger fiddled with the fabric of her hem, and she added, "I don't want to go."

"Why not?" Arthur held his breath because this answer was important to him, too.

"I want to love the man I marry. I don't want to marry someone because he is rich and famous," Rose blurted and turned her eyes to Arthur.

Arthur's gaze moved from her eyes to her lips, and he wanted to kiss her so much. He turned his eyes away and said, "If you don't want to go, can you tell your father that?"

Aislinn shook her head. "No, he wouldn't listen to me. He would say I have never been to London, and that it will be a great experience and that I will love seeing all the sights and meeting new people."

"What can you do?" Arthur asked.

"I don't know. I only know I don't want to get married this summer." Rose frowned and then turned to him. "How are you doing, Arthur?"

He glanced at his big, callused hands. He had worked hard and learned his profession as a gardener. He loved flowers. "I've been keeping your father's garden in good shape. I planted more flowers and brushes." He pointed out the rose vines and added, "The climbing roses are especially beautiful this year."

Rose kept her eyes on him. "You do what you love."

Arthur faced her. "Yes, I love gardening." He paused. He wanted to tell her his secret project.

She leaned on and touched Arthur's hand. "What is it? Tell me."

"Can you keep a secret?" Arthur looked serious.

"Yes, of course," Rose replied.

This is getting interesting, she thought. *Arthur has a secret. I hope it's not a girlfriend.* And when she thought about that, she felt a pang of jealousy inside her.

She did not have time to further inspect her feelings because Arthur said, "I have a secret project. I cultivate new roses, which are more beautiful and different than anyone has seen. Some are more disease resistant, and some have different shades of colors like white with pink edges."

Rose raised her eyebrows. "Why do you do that?"

Arthur smiled and relaxed. "I want to participate in a rose competition. The roses are judged on various criteria ranging from overall garden presentation to disease resistance and the presence of fragrance."

"And you want to create a prize-winning rose!" Rose said, happily clapping her hands together.

"Yes, I do. I have a couple of good prospects now, and I plan to enter them in a competition soon," Arthur replied, leaning back against the pavilion pole.

"That is so wonderful!" Rose said, and she tilted her head and asked, "What can you win in a flower competition? Are there monetary prizes?"

Arthur stared into the distance. "The Royal Society arranged the best competition, and they announced a new one. The first prize is twenty-five thousand pounds. I want to take my roses there. If I win, the queen herself will hand out the prize, and the chosen flowers will be planted in her royal garden."

"Twenty-five thousand pounds! That's a fortune!" Rose stared at him with wide eyes. "I didn't know growing roses could be so lucrative."

Arthur smiled and nodded. "Not all the roses are, but some are worth more than you think." And he was right: a new rose would be worth a fortune because many noble families would want to have a winning rose in their garden. He would be busy creating and delivering his roses after winning a competition like that.

"I hope you're right. Are you sure your roses are good enough? They sure are beautiful," Rose commented, glancing around.

"Yes, I'm sure they are," Arthur replied. He knew his trade, and he had made the wining roses, he was sure.

CHAPTER FIVE

Arthur's Roses

"I want to see your project, Arthur. Show me!" Rose demanded. She stood up and brushed her light summer dress with her hands. She didn't want it to get dirty because if her mother saw her brand-new dress stained and wrinkled, she would definitely reprimand her.

Arthur got up slowly, wondering if it had been a good idea to tell Rose about her project. When he glanced at her, Arthur saw only excitement. Her eyes sparkled like two stars as she took his hand and stepped out of the pavilion. Arthur pulled his hand away. It was not proper for a duke's daughter to go hand in hand with a gardener.

Arthur led her to a path she didn't even know existed, and Rose was surprised to find that the garden was rather large, hiding behind a patch of maple trees and tall brushes. The garden had a couple of small outbuildings, well-maintained lush green lawns, and many flowers, not just roses and lilacs.

Hurriedly, the couple made their way along a neat stone path, which twisted and turned, and in no time at all, they were near a glass-walled greenhouse with open windows. She followed Arthur inside and found rows of terracotta pots, each of them filled with roses.

Arthur gestured at them. "These are my roses. Each one of them is different in the color and size of the bloom. Some have thorns, and others don't. Some of these roses are climbers, and some are great as cut flowers. For example, this one. I call it my Magnificent Rose." He strolled to one of the bushes with big roses, picked up pruners from the table, cut a beautiful crimson red rose, and handed it to Rose.

Rose took her flower, sniffed it, and said, "It is magnificent. It looks perfect."

Perfect like you, Arthur thought as he admired the young lady in front of her.

When Rose turned her amethyst-blue eyes to him, Arthur could not help but tell her, "Rose, I love you."

She smiled and said, "I know." She gazed downwards. "I don't think my father will let you marry me. His mind is set on marrying me to some stranger with loads of money."

Arthur grabbed her hand and said fiercely, "I will have money soon. I will win the competition, then I can open my flower shop. I could earn more money by selling flowers and arranging flowers for parties and ton's households than I can as a gardener. "

Rose turned her head and pulled away from her hand. "You would be a merchant, not a lord or a baron. My parents would never let me marry someone below my societal class. As a merchant, you would be a member of the middle class, and I would still be a daughter of a duke. Our marriage is nothing more than a dream."

Arthur grabbed her by the shoulders and turned her towards him. She kept her eyes downwards. Arthur gently lifted her chin so she had to face him. "I will make it happen. Will you wait for me?"

Rose assessed the young, handsome man in front of him without knowing what she should say. He was always dressed in cream-colored breeches and polished black knee boots. He had a white shirt and a tan-colored vest over it. Rose was once again struck by his ha and symmetrical features. If Arthur had been a son of an upper-class family, Rose's father would have been glad to give her hand to him. Arthur was a man of his word. He was trustworthy and loyal, and he was a diligent worker. However, there was nothing Rose could do to convince her father to let her marry him. She knew that and realized she would not want to marry anyone else but him. They belonged together.

Rose sighed. "I will do my best to avoid marriage. I don't have to accept any proposals this summer. One day, my father will expect me to marry someone important." She batted her eyelashes and added, "I love you, Arthur."

He pulled her closer and kissed her passionately. It was Rose's first kiss, and it was all she had ever dreamed of. She could feel her heart beating in her throat. She lifted her arms around Arthur's neck and kissed him back. Arthur slid his hands firmly around her waist, drawing Rose's body closer to his. Rose dug her fingers into his thick hair and lightly twisted it around her fingers, enjoying the feel of it against her fingers. As their kiss became longer and more fervent, Arthur tightened his grip on her waist, and Rose suddenly realized they were in a greenhouse where any servant or her parents could walk in and discover the two of them. She sighed, placed both hands on his chest, and gently pushed him away.

Suddenly, her passion waned, and it was replaced by sheer panic. She glanced around to make sure they were still alone, and she took a few steps backward to ensure she was not too close to Arthur. For several seconds, Arthur and Rose simply stood there staring into each other's eyes, both of them a little shocked by their strong feelings. They both realized that something had happened which could not be taken back, and they had broken the rules of good manners: a duke's daughter kissing a servant!

Rose considered what would happen if her parents found out about the two of them. What if she and the gardener were to be discovered, and became the target of gossip? That would be awful. She raised her hand to her neck and shook her head. "We can't be seen doing this. We must find a way to solve our problem."

Arthur gave her a crooked smile. "Love is not a problem."

"No, but the societal rules and classes are, and you know it. I can't be seen kissing a servant in my father's household," Rose snapped. Her eyes turned darker with emotion.

Arthur was taken aback by her harsh comment. She was right, though. Arthur knew his love was not appropriate. He would have to figure out a way to make it proper. The first step would be the rose competition.

Rose looked pensive.

"What is it?" Arthur asked.

"If we could find out who your real parents were, perhaps that would be helpful," Rose replied quietly.

"I don't know anything about them," Arthur said, his eyes turning cold. He had often thought about who his parents had been and why he was abandoned to live on the streets of London. Didn't his parents love him? Were they too poor to take care of him? He knew nothing of them.

"That's what I'm saying. We need to find out who they were and what happened to you," Rose insisted. She had a hunch that Arthur, with his manners and wit, was not simply a son of a prostitute or a fisherman. She was sure there was more—

CHAPTER SIX

A Trip to London

Aislinn had organized their trip to London swiftly.

Her father, George Ackley, and his wife, Lady Olivia, had sent a note that they would be pleased to meet them after they had settled i n.

Rose wore a simple blue cotton travel dress with a blue bonnet decorated with tiny white flowers. She grabbed the windowsill of the carriage and stared outside. She was not interested in going to London, attending balls, or meeting numerous gents. Rose would have been happy in her father's estate with Arthur. She knew that wouldn't be possible, so she did what was asked and got ready for the season of balls.

It was a sunny spring day, and the sky was clear. Rose's mind was still pondering Arthur's past. How could she find out where he had come from? Then she remembered the old butler, Mattson. He was now in their London residence, and she remembered her father telling her how he had taken care of Arthur while her mother and Lord Ackley were arrested and Duke Ian was in a hurry to find the real assassins and rescue the love of his life, Aislinn.

Rose straightened up in her seat. Perhaps, Mattson could tell her something more about Arthur.

Aislinn, noticing how Rose looked more alert, said, "This trip has been exhausting. I'm sure you will be happy to get to London and rest for a while." Aislinn brushed the long hem of her navy-blue travel dress and sighed. "I don't go to London often because I hate the dusty, bumpy roads. It's been a year since my last visit."

Rose nodded, agreeing. "Yes, mama. I can't wait to get there," Rose replied, although she had different reasons than what her mother imagined.

"Lady Olivia can't wait to see what a perfect lady you've become. She will take you to a dressmaker and get you more dresses fit for dancing."

"I have plenty of dresses. Lillian made me a dozen with the same high-waist model. I'm sure I can't wear more dresses in one season!" Rose complained.

"The ball dresses are nowadays made of a heavier fabric. The ones you have now are perfect for a walk in a park or to visit other ton families during the day. They are not dancing dresses," Aislinn explained. She knew it well. She had got new dresses in London when she was a debutante. She remembered how she had to adjust to Lady Olivia's strict daily training, the dance lessons, her dressmaker's pinches, and her hairdresser's miracle work with her hairdo.

"Oh, I see," Rose replied and glanced outside. London's houses were visible on the horizon. It wouldn't take long to reach the outskirts of the city. She remembered visiting London when she was a child, but not lately. She was curious to see if her memories would match the current cityscape. She recalled gas lights on the streets, narrow roads, tightly built rows of houses, more expensive-looking and bigger mansions in the area where her father's London residence was, and shabbier and poorly built houses on the fringes of the city limits.

Rose preferred the open space, the green grass, and the flowers in their estate. She had no interest in staying in London longer than was necessary. She wanted to show her parents that she had done what they asked, attended the parties, and met new people, but no one would force her to accept any gent to be her husband, not even her father, Duke Ian.

CHAPTER SEVEN

London Townhouse

When the carriage stopped in front of the duke's townhouse, Aislinn was greeted by Mattson, the duke's lifetime butler who had known Arthur as a street urchin. Rose stepped down and waited for her mother to finish asking all the pertinent questions like "Was the house warmed? Were the rooms aired? Is the kitchen ready to entertain them and their guests?" And so on.

Mattson replied to all her questions, "Yes, milady." He had taken care of the duke's parents here before they gave the house to Ian, and after Ian's marriage, he had continued his service dutifully.

Mattson adored Ian when he was a child, and he loved to take care of him and his family whenever they visited London.

Rose let all her mother's questions relating to the household pass as she viewed the street. It was as she remembered: This street had larger brick houses with lawns and bushes in front of the building. It meant the more affluent members of the society lived here, those who were members of the House of Lords.

Rose waited for his mother to finish her questions, and then they ambled inside. Mattson stayed behind, taking care of the carriage and the luggage. Rose decided to catch him later when she was alone, and her mother would not hear what she wanted to ask.

Aislinn stopped by the hallway table and saw a stack of invitations to balls and tea with biscuits. She exclaimed happily, "Look how many invitations! Lady Olivia must have told everyone we were coming! How nice. I must write to each of these people, and we'll see how busy our schedule will be. First, I want to see Lady Olivia and my father."

She called for a servant and asked, "Can you take a message to my father and ask if they could see Rose and me today? We could arrive at their home at teatime. Thank you." The servant nodded and rushed to take care of the message.

Rose groaned. She had hoped for a free afternoon and evening, but it looked like her mother had other thoughts.

Aislinn ushered her to change her travel clothes before having a snack with her downstairs, so they both walked upstairs to refresh, then returned to the dining room for a light snack which included bacon, eggs, and a toast with jam. They had traveled for many hours, so they were both hungry.

Aislinn was the first to enter the dining room. Her day dress was a lilac-colored cotton dress with darker purple decorations. It brought up her eye color and made them look deeper and darker. Her hair was tied up, and she had a small flower and pearl decoration on her bun.

Dressed in a lemon-yellow chiffon dress as was befitting for a young lady, Rose sauntered into the dining room through the arched doorway, her mahogany tresses tied back into a bun and her face looking pale.

For a long moment, Aislinn's eyes lingered on Rose's face. Aislinn suspected something because Rose didn't seem excited to be in London and become a debutante this summer.

Perhaps, I am overthinking, she thought. *It might be the long trip making Rose look exhausted. But she will have to get back her rosy cheeks if she wants to get a husband this summer,* Aislinn contemplated.

Rose sat beside her, and the servant brought her a plate with bacon and eggs. She was exceptionally quiet, so Aislinn decided to ask, "Are you feeling well, dear?"

Rose glanced up. "Yes, I'm fine. Only tired. The carriage ride was long and exhausting."

"Good, because we have a lot to do in London. Do you think you can accompany me to see your grandfather and Lady Olivia?" Aislinn kept her eyes on her daughter and noted she did not eat much but just moved the food on her plate to make it look like she had eaten.

Lifting her head, Rose replied, "Yes, I'd love to see them. It's been almost a year since I saw them last time."

Aislinn gestured to Rose's plate and said, "If you don't want to eat that, I'm sure the kitchen can make you something else."

Rose lowered her hands on her lap and said, "I think I could just have some toast and jam with a cup of tea, please?"

The servant nodded and took away her plate with eggs and bacon. She had not eaten any of it. Soon, the servant returned with another plate with toast and jam.

The bread was white and fresh, and Rose could smell it. She spread the raspberry jam on it and took a bite. It was heavenly. She loved the taste and smell of fresh white bread.

Aislinn smiled and commented, "That looks better."

Rose nodded back and said, "It tastes so good."

A servant came in and handed Aislinn a note from Lady Olivia. Aislinn's face brightened as she read it. "We can go there right away after we've finished eating. They are anxious to see us, and Lady Olivia has some gossip to tell us, too. I can't wait to hear what she has heard. I bet she has news about all the eligible bachelors in London!"

After their snack, Aislinn asked Mattson to bring the carriage in front of the house, and they headed to meet Lord Ackley and Lady Olivia.

Rose was eager to see her grandfather and his second wife, Lady Olivia. They were always kind to her and adored her, as she was Aislinn's only child. They lived in Lady Olivia's townhouse, which was as large as the duke's residence. Lady Olivia was wealthy because of her first marriage, and marrying Lord Ackley had not reduced her income from her first husband's estates. Lord Ackley loved her more than his own life, and she had given him the son he always had secretly wanted. Andre was about the same age as Rose, and they used to play together as children.

When they arrived at their destination, the carriage stopped, and they stepped down to a paved sidewalk. The servant opened a door, and they strolled inside. They didn't have to introduce themselves, as Lord Ackley and his wife were both in the hallway greeting and hugging them. Lady Olivia wore a bright green day dress with a wide hem decorated with expensive-looking lace. Her hair was tied in a bun on her neck.

She gave Rose a quick assessing glance from top to toe. "You look beautiful but too shy. Men like livelier ladies and spunk in the young debutantes. But don't worry, we'll get you a husband soon."

Rose winced. That was not what she wanted. "I'm grateful for your help, Aunt Olivia." She hated being shown around as a gift to eligible aristocrats. That was not what she wanted.

"First, we have to get rid of the lemon-yellow dress. It seems to take the color out of you!" Lady Olivia announced.

Rose dropped her gaze and let it sweep down over her gown. She liked the dress, but perhaps it was too pale. Her skin was creamy colored, but this dress made it look ghastly white.

After greeting her daughter and granddaughter, Lord Ackley sneaked out, as he didn't want to listen to the eternal gossiping between the ladies.

Eventually, Rose spent all day listening to her mother and Lady Olivia. Lady Olivia had so much to tell them! She knew all the important ton gossip, including who was available this season, who had gotten married, widowed, and who was out of town now. Aislinn was more engaged in this conversation than her daughter.

Aislinn found herself drawn into one conversation after another about who could be a suitable match for Rose and how Rose was to procure his attention. They spent hours at Lady Olivia's discussing the possible dressmakers, what hairstyle was in style this season, and which balls were the most important ones to attend.

Lady Olivia also revealed who she thought was Rose's biggest competition this season: The first one was Susan Farrington, the daughter of Baron Farrington, as she was both wealthy and fairly pretty, and the second was Janet Cambert, the daughter of Lord Cambert, and she was also from a rich and old family.

Rose's head spun by the time evening fell, and they returned to their London residence.

CHAPTER EIGHT

Rose and Mattson

Finally, the first day in London was over. Rose was overwhelmed with the gossip and plans Lady Olivia and her mother had laid out for her: How to entice a gentleman when there are many debutantes, how to flirt, and how to attract the possible suitors at the ball. She was happy to retire to her room for the evening and asked to have a small dinner plate brought to her.

She stretched out on her bed and sighed. As much as she wanted to ignore her mother's attempts to get her engaged, she would not be swayed. She knew her mother would not hear her objections—as feeble as they were—because she was happily married and wanted the same for her daughter.

The last discussion with Lady Olivia was how to doll her up for the first ball: her hair would be braided and twirled into a bun on top of her head and decorated with pearls and flowers. Her dress would be light pink with darker red embroidery. The collar of her dress would be low enough to show the cleavage, and her sleeves would be short and puffy. She felt like a doll being dressed and wanted to protest with vehemence, to argue against their plans, but she could not. Not without revealing her true love and what her real plans were.

Most of all, she needed to speak to Mattson because the butler might remember more about Arthur, where he used to live in London when he was a street urchin, and where she could find his previous friends, relatives, or parents. Rose waited for her dinner plate, ate the fish and chips in a hurry, then quietly opened her room and sauntered downstairs. She avoided the dining room in case her mother was dining there and instead went to the living room and asked the servant if Mattson could come and see her.

Mattson arrived soon after, and Rose faced her with a newfound determination. "Mattson, you were my father's butler before he married."

He gave her a quizzical look but answered, "Yes, Miss Rose. I have served your father and his family all his life."

Rose fiddled her hem with her fingers and said, "You met Arthur Smith as a young boy. He was the one who helped you and my father to save my mother from Tower prison."

Mattson placed his hands behind his back, and his face remained unemotional as he answered, "Yes, that is correct, Miss Rose."

Rose took a step closer and asked, "Do you remember anything about Arthur's past? Where did he live or stay? Who were his friends? Who would know more about his past?"

Ah, that's what Miss Rose is after, Mattson thought. He frowned. "Miss Rose, if Arthur has done something wrong, I should take that up with your father. The duke does not like the servants to make advances to his daughter."

Rose paled. *Oh, no. He misunderstood me.* She stepped closer, reached out for Mattson's hand, and grabbed it. "Please, don't tell my father anything. I just want to learn more about Arthur and his past." She stared at the old butler with pleading eyes and added, "Arthur has been a perfect gentleman. He has not done anything wrong. Don't mention my questions to my mother either."

Mattson pulled his hand from Rose's grip and replied politely, "Miss Rose, this question is strange. May I inquire why you want to know more about Arthur?"

Rose sighed. "Yes, of course." She looked at him, assessing if she could trust him. "I'm going to tell you something that no one else knows. You must promise me that you will keep it a secret."

Mattson replied, "Miss Rose, I won't tell a soul—unless it will damage your father's reputation or this family."

Rose glanced at him. He looked honest and trustworthy, so she decided to tell him what was bothering her. "You can't tell my father or my mother. I plan to marry Arthur. It would be easier if I knew more about him. I know we were not born in the same social class, but I don't care. I love him, and he loves me."

Oh no, Mattson thought and lifted his hand to rub his forehead. This was even worse than he had expected: it could ruin this family's reputation, and the duke would be furious if he found out about it. *What can I do or say?*

She waited for him to answer. Finally, he decided to level with her. "Miss Rose, your plan is preposterous. You're a wealthy heiress of a duke. He will be a formidable enemy if he gets angry with Arthur. He will ruin him. You can't let that happen. I'm not going to help you to ruin your life or Arthur's."

Mattson was about to leave the room when Rose said quietly, "Mattson, if you love this family, you will tell me anything and everything you know about Arthur. He is a decent man. He will get rich. When he does, he can marry me. I don't care about the titles. If he is successful in his business, he can buy a title. You can't mention any of this to my parents. It is better if they don't get worried or angry."

Mattson stared at the young lady in front of him. He realized Rose was much like his father, Ian, at that moment. He remembered well when Ian had decided to save Aislinn and her father from Tower's prison, and he had no idea how to do that. He managed to find the real assassins and save her future wife. Ian was as determined then as Rose was now. Mattson knew that he had to help Rose, or she would go out and get into trouble. She didn't know all the dangers of London's streets and alleys. She could get hurt, and then the duke would be beside himself and blame the household for letting that happen. Mattson realized he had only one choice: Help Rose find out more about Arthur.

He took a deep breath and replied, "Miss Rose, I will try to find out more about Arthur as you asked. Please, don't do anything that your father would not approve of. Ask me first, and I will assist you."

Rose hugged Mattson and surprised him. "Thank you! Thank you! You are the best butler ever!" She danced happily out of the room.

Mattson sighed. Like father, like daughter.

CHAPTER NINE

Roses and Dreams

While Rose was in London with her mother, Arthur continued his gardener work and dreamt of his own business as a florist and a flower merchant.

He had not hidden his projects from the duke and his family. Everyone knew he had a special interest in flowers, so the duke allowed him to turn this greenhouse into a rose breeding zone. He had even encouraged Arthur to go after his dream, and obviously, he had a talent for it.

Arthur knew he would succeed if he got the seed money, which he would get by winning a rose competition announced by the Royal Society. The first prize, twenty-five thousand, would be more than enough to start a business in two locations and get the inventory. He would earn enough money to court Rose if the duke allowed it. He would not be an aristocrat. That was the biggest problem. He could not buy a title in England. The Queen was the only one who could grant you a title. In Germany, they allowed purchasing titles, but he didn't know how much they would cost or if it would be worth the trouble to do that. Would a title mean that much to Duke Ian?

After finishing his duties in the garden, Arthur went to his greenhouse to continue his project with roses. He had decided to send three roses to the competition. His first choice was the Sunrise Rose, a vibrant yellow rose with a hint of orange on the petals. It was a large rose with about thirty petals and around five inches in size when fully opened. Its irresistible lemon scent was the one that made it different from the other yellow roses. His second choice was Ackley's Dream, a classic white rose with a hint of pink inside and a fruity fragrance. His favorite was the Magnificent Rose, which had the deepest crimson buds when it opened, and the flower size was around five inches with forty petals of velvety dark red. Fully opened, the rose revealed a large center with the most beautiful rich golden stamens, and its fragrance reminded him of summer berries.

He had packed his best specimen in a box and was ready to ship them to the judges of the Royal Society. He had carefully ensured that the flowers would not suffer in packaging and tried to put both moisture and room for the plants so that they would not suffer during the trip.

He heard steps by the doorway and turned around to see Duke Ian ambling toward him. He stopped by his working area and noted what he was doing.

"What are you packing?" the duke asked as he saw how carefully Arthur carried and packed the roses.

"I have decided to participate in a rose competition. The Royal Society has announced it, and I think my roses are worth sending there." Arthur looked up to the duke and added, "They are unique. No one can breed them like I do, sir."

Duke Ian nodded. "Yes, they are exquisite. I've never seen such vibrant colors, and they have beautiful fragrances, too." He glanced at the box and asked, "Aren't these flowers going to wilt or be damaged during the trip?"

Arthur stared at the worktable and then turned to face Duke Ian. "Yes, sir. That's possible. I'll try to pack them as well as I can."

Duke Ian put his hand on Arthur's shoulder and said, "I think you should take the trip with the plants to make sure they are delivered in good condition. We'll manage here without you for a while. Your work with them has taken time and effort, and you should see what it is worth. I'll ask my driver to take you to the competition, and you can stay in London in my townhouse." Then he remembered that his daughter and his wife were there, too, and added, "I better go along with you. I wouldn't mind spending some time with my family, too. I miss them."

Arthur was at a loss for words. He opened and closed his mouth. "Duke, sir... You're taking me to London? I can participate in the competition?"

Duke Ian smiled. "Yes, you can. We have to make sure you are presentable there. I'll ask my tailor to make something for you to wear. You can't go there as a servant. You must look the part. No one will take you seriously if you look like a gardener. I think I should attend the competition with you to make sure they all respect you."

It will be better than attending the balls and sipping tea at the parties in London, Ian thought.

CHAPTER TEN

The First Ball

"The first ball of the season! How exciting!" Aislinn exclaimed enthusiastically and clapped her hands together as if she was the debutante instead of her daughter. She wore a lavender blue high-waist dress with a choker made of pearls and amethysts and a matching set of earrings.

The first ball of the season was held at the Viscount Arlington's townhouse this year. Rose had never met them, but Lady Olivia had talked about them as if they were her good friends.

Rose descended calmly down the stairs and locked her calm eyes with her mother's. "Rose, you look absolutely beautiful!" Her mother walked to her side and admired her hairdo and her dress.

Rose gave a stiff smile and said, "Should we go now? I don't want us to be late."

"Yes, of course. The carriage is ready." Aislinn rushed to the door, where the servant waited to help them to climb up into the carriage. Rose followed, showing less interest in going to the ball.

Rose had a couple of ideas about what she could do at the ball if someone showed interest in her because she had no intention of pleasing any gentleman.

Lady Olivia's dressmaker had created a stunning ball dress for her, and Lillian had helped her with her hairdo. Rose's hair had been styled so that it was smooth on the right side and held there with pearly pins and pink flowers, and on the left side, her thick, golden-brown locks were curling temptingly over her shoulder.

Rose wore a light pink dress with a long train, the color more befitting to her complexion and hair color than the previous lemon hue she had worn when she met her grandfather and Lady Olivia. Her dress had a fashionably low square neckline, drawing eyes to her exposed long neck and the line between her breasts. She felt that men would stare at her neckline in that dress, but Lady Olivia had insisted the neckline should be low this season; otherwise, she would not be able to compete with the other debutantes. Rose rolled her eyes behind Lady Olivia's back! As if Rose cared about any of that...

Long white gloves covered her hands, and in her pink purse was the rose from Arthur, which she always carried with her. Arthur was always on her mind. She couldn't help herself. She was in love.

Rose's dress train was rounded at the end, and the hem was finished with a lace and silk ruffle. Rose had also complained about the length of it because she was sure it would make her trip, and if not her, then one of the potential gents. But then that gave her an idea of how to avoid possible admirers.

Rose let out a soft, breathy sigh when she listened to her mother's enthusiastic chatting in the carriage. They would meet Lady Olivia at the ball. She wanted to witness her granddaughter's success at the ball.

When they arrived at Arlington's house, the yard was lit with dozens of lights, and they heard music and laughter echoing from inside the fully lit house through the open windows and doorways. Their carriage had to wait for its turn because several carriages were queuing in front of them. It wasn't easy to climb down from the carriages with heavy muslin skirts with long trains and the dress's fabric draped up into a bell shape with an abundance of flounces.

Rose almost laughed when she saw a few older ladies with huge busts and the back of their ball dresses formed into massive fashionable bustles, dropping to a long train. With their trendily wide dresses, they had difficulty getting out of their carriages. She realized Lady Olivia had been correct in choosing her dress because all the other women had similar styles, including long dress trains, and all their silhouettes were alike: narrow waists, tight bodices, and wide overskirts.

When their carriage finally reached the front, Aislinn stepped out first, and then Rose gathered her train in her hand before carefully stepping down from the carriage. She took a deep breath as she stood in front of the lit two-floor brick building and saw the gathering of society's finest in the yard, on the balcony, and on the wide terrace.

She followed her mother inside, where they were greeted by an elderly couple. The servant introduced them to the host and hostess: "Duchess Aislinn Manchester and her daughter Rose."

Rose curtsied slightly as she greeted the host, the hostess, and their daughter, who was about the same age as Rose. *Another debutante*, she thought and groaned inwardly. The daughter, Vivian, was so shy she hid behind her mother's back when the guests kept entering the hall. She looked so uncomfortable in her wide red dress. *She probably would have preferred a different color dress with fewer ruffles and bows*, Rose thought, feeling sorry for Vivian. Rose smiled at Vivian when their eyes met, and she winced and smiled back. *She seems to agree that these dresses are so uncomfortable*, Rose thought, grimacing.

Aislinn and Rose moved forward to let other guests in. Aislinn led her to Lady Olivia, sitting with the married ladies by the dance floor. "Oh, Rose, you look adorable." Lady Olivia said and then introduced her to the mothers and daughters, including her greatest competitors this season: Susan Farrington and Janet Cambert. Rose smiled at everyone while the mothers of the debutantes assessed her as a serious competitor in the marriage market.

Rose didn't care. She was more interested in the decorations of the ballroom. Her gaze roamed the room and saw the multiplicity of candles placed around the ballroom and the extravagant flower arrangements. Her eyes latched on the narrow tables with flower centerpieces and some fashionable snacks like biscuits and muffins. She nudged her mother and asked, "Could I go and get something to eat? I'm hungry."

"Yes, dear. Let's go before they run out of snacks. We can also get something to drink." Aislinn led her away from the women's group and whispered, "I think you have nothing to fear. None of those girls is any match to your beauty."

Rose sighed again. She didn't want to be the belle of the ball.

But before Rose had a chance to get a plate with a biscuit, she heard a familiar voice behind her, "May I ask your daughter to dance, Lady Aislinn?"

When Rose and her mother turned around, Aislinn recognized Andre, her stepbrother from her father's second marriage with Lady Olivia.

"Andre! I was hoping to see you here." Aislinn gave her stepbrother a light hug.

"Of course, I'm here. My mother would not let me pass any of these events," Andre replied and winked at Rose, who smiled. Andre was born the same year as Rose.

Aislinn retorted, "You look so dashing!" Andre's hair was dark brown, his eyes dark brown, and he wore a black tailcoat, a blue silk waistcoat, long white pants, and he had bushy sideburns, which was the style with men now. "Go on to dance. It's a good place for you two to show off your talents."

Gracefully, Andre led Rose to the dance floor. And because they were close relatives, Rose didn't have to pretend with him. She could actually enjoy the first dance. As many gentlemen were present, she hoped they would pick some of the other debutantes and let her be alone.

The first dance was a waltz, which Rose had learned at the boarding school. She gathered her train on her arm so it would not be on the way when they danced.

"How do you like the ball?" Andre asked at the dance floor.

"It's interesting," Aislinn replied. She had never danced with a man in a public event before. At the boarding school, the dance lessons were between girls, and no men were allowed to be present. She was, therefore, happy that the first dance was with Andre.

"I did not mean that." The movement of the dance drew them to the other end of the ballroom. Andre added, "I can't seem to envision you chasing a husband at the ball. It's not your style. I think you're headstrong like your father and your mother. You want to choose by yourself and not let your mother or my mother dictate your fate. That is all."

Rose nodded and half-closed her eyes as the music flowed in the air, and she followed Andre's firm guidance through the floor. "You're right. I wouldn't like that."

Andre furrowed his brows. "Is there something I should know? Do you have a beau?"

Rose blushed. "I can't tell you. You might tell my mother and your mother about him."

Andre pulled her closer. "Never. I keep secrets better than any woman I know."

Rose sighed. "I don't plan to marry any gentleman in London even though that's my parents' wish. I have met someone I love and want to marry him."

"Why don't you?"

Rose looked sad. "He is not suitable. He is not an aristocrat."

Andre laughed. "Oh my! Rose!" he whispered in her ear. "I will keep your secret, and if I can, I will help you to avoid the marriage proposals this summer."

Rose nodded and smiled at him. "Thank you, Andre. You're my best friend."

"I wish I could be there when your father finds out who you're in love with," he replied, grinning.

"It will take some time before I can tell him that. You see, the man I love has a plan, but it will take months or even a year before he can propose to me. Meanwhile, I need to find out more about him and his past." Rose looked Andre in the eyes.

Andre tilted his head. "He does not know who he is?"

"No, he is an orphan. That's why I need more time to find out who he is and where he came from."

"Let me guess: I bet I have met him. He works for your father, and he is the one who saved my father and your mother from Tower. Did I guess correctly?" Andre's eyes drilled into Rose's.

Rose blushed and replied, "Yes, you've guessed who he is."

Andre nodded. His voice was serious when he replied, "He's a good man. I hope everything works out for you two."

When the first dance ended, Andre led Rose back to her mother, who was now talking with Lady Olivia. They had tried to eavesdrop on the other mothers to find out what they thought about Rose and Andre. They seemed to be very pleased with what they had heard.

Chapter Eleven

Rose at the Ball

Andre stood by Rose after the dance. He noticed several men gave her admiring glances. Rose was a beauty, even if she didn't want to find a husband here. Her light pink dress enhanced the color of her skin, making it look glowing.

Vivian, the hostess's daughter, was still a wallflower, looking sad, and Rose decided it was time for Andre to help. "Ask Vivian to dance, please."

She turned her pleading eyes to Andre, who sighed and nodded. "Okay, I can do one good deed here."

Andre glanced at the girl trying to hide behind her mother again and rolled his eyes. He whispered to Rose, "She looks hideous in that dark red dress. That color is good for someone older and with darker hair. Whoever dresses her does not know anything about what suits her. Those ruffles are dreadful."

Rose poked him with her elbow. "Go! Now!"

"I will, I will," Andre grumbled.

He approached Vivian, bowed before her, and asked her to dance. She blushed, and her face turned the color of beet. She didn't know what to say. Andre gave his hand, and they walked away to dance. Rose smiled victoriously. Good, Vivian seemed nice, although she was awfully shy. As she observed the couple dancing, she noted that Vivian was not a bad dancer. Andre had an easy time leading her on the dance fl oor.

Aislinn, Rose's mother, reminisced about her first ball and how she met her husband, Ian, the Duke of Manchester. The memory of the ball was vivid in her mind, as was the awful experiment in the Tower prison when she and her father had been suspected of the queen's assassination. She sighed. It is all past now.

She glanced around the dance hall: the alabaster Greek statues placed around the room, the magnificent flower arrangements artfully decorating the tables on the wall side, and the smell of candles mixing with the various perfumes and all the gossiping with the other mothers made her thrilled. I hope Rose finds a husband here, she thought, her eyes sparkling.

Meanwhile, Rose casually surveyed the room. She saw men assessing her, felt sweat pool in her armpits, and wished she could run away. Her dancing card was still empty after Andre, but she was not worried, for she knew her mother would not let her be a wallflower, and she would introduce Rose to eligible gentlemen to dance with. She wished no one would come and ask her to dance. Her heart belonged to Arthur. Only Andre knew her secret and Mattson too.

Rose glanced at her mother standing by the side, busily chatting with a group of ladies. She tapped her pink slipper on the floor along the beat of the music, swayed a bit, and watched the couples form on the dance floor. She loved dancing and wished she could join them, but that would mean courting another man. That would be risky! Perhaps Andre would ask her to dance again...

Then he appeared out of nowhere! A stranger in his black coat and a silk shirt, with thick, wavy blond hair, a double chin, a potbelly, and cold blue eyes. He had a slight smile on his lips when he bowed and asked her to dance. "Rose, the daughter of Duke Manchester," Rose heard her mother introducing her to this stranger. "This gentleman here is Viscount Gerald Smythe. His father is the Earl of Chesterton."

Rose curtsied. Her wide pink dress surrounded her like a rose blossom. She was a beautiful sight.

"May I ask for this dance?" His voice had a nasal sound, and he looked at Rose as if she were a specimen on a microscope. Rose didn't want to dance with him, but she didn't want to be impolite in front of the mothers.

Rose's heart quickened as she took his arm, and he led her to the dance floor. This is the moment to show the other men that she was not worth wooing, Rose thought.

Now, it is time for action, she thought. She dropped her train from her hand, "Oh," she mumbled and then leaned to grab it, but at the same time, stumbled against Viscount Smythe, making him take a few steps backward and hitting the dancing couples behind him. They all fell to the floor.

Rose lifted her hand over her mouth, not to giggle. She had to take a deep breath to calm herself. This went better than I had planned.

Other couples stopped dancing, and the men helped the couple and Viscount Smythe back up from the floor. He wiped his clothes with his hand and turned his icy eyes on Rose, his face red from anger and humiliation. "Shall we continue, Miss Rose?"

The music continued.

Rose nodded. She placed her hand on his shoulder, and he put his sweaty palm on her waist. They started the dance in two steps, but Rose tripped on her feet and stepped on his left foot on purpose. "Oh, I'm so sorry!" she apologized.

He limped and stopped dancing. "Perhaps, we can skip this dance, Miss Rose. I don't think I'm quite ready for more." He grabbed her by the arm and led her back to Aislinn, who raised her eyebrows but didn't comment until Viscount Smythe left their company.

Then she pulled Rose aside and asked, "What was that all about, Rose?" Her eyes were sharp as she looked into her daughter's.

"The floor was slippery. I stumbled, that's all, mother." Rose shrugged. Inside, she was pleased with her plan. No one would ask her to dance for a while when they saw how clumsy she was with the viscount.

Andre returned with Vivian, bowed to her, and left her with her mother. He returned to Rose's side and whispered, "Is that your plan: to make all the suitors limp away from you?"

He chuckled as Rose turned her innocent eyes to him and replied, "I have no idea what you're talking about, Andre."

"Remember, they saw you waltz with me. They know you can dance that one. You're not safe yet," Andre replied smugly.

Rose frowned. He was right. She had waltzed with him without any trouble. She had to figure out something else for the next suitor.

"Mother, can we go and get something to eat?" she asked.

Aislinn nodded. "Yes, I think that's a great idea. Especially after your last performance."

Rose winced. Her mother was suspicious. She'd have to be careful how she proceeded. They went to the table with biscuits and cakes. Aislinn chose a piece of raspberry tart, whereas Rose picked a red velvet cake. They ambled to the side of the table and started eating when another gentleman approached and bowed. "May I have this dance?"

He was a heavyset man with hands as large as loaves of bread. His eyes were squinty, and he had an ill-fitting white wig on top of his head, showing his dark hair under it. Rose took a step forward and accidentally tripped. Her cake flew on the suitor's white shirt.

"Oh!" Rose sighed as she watched the cake stain his vest and shirt.

"Excuse me," the suitor said, quickly bowed, and disappeared from their sight.

"You're unusually clumsy today," Aislinn said.

"These new slippers are slippery," Rose muttered. She turned and picked a new plate and a piece of cake. She was pleased with her results at the ball.

The evening went by, and no other admirers approached Rose to dance. She was excited to watch the other couples on the dance floor. When it was time to leave, Aislinn said, "Let me say goodbye to our hostess and find Lady Olivia."

Rose waited for the two ladies to arrive, and they left together.

Lady Olivia gazed at Aislinn and commented, "You had some mishaps, Rose. I hope the next ball goes better. I don't think you made anyone lose their heart to you tonight."

"I know, auntie. I was nervous, I guess." Rose smiled coyly at Lady Olivia. Andre winked at her behind his mother when she wasn't looking.

Rose smiled at him. He knew her secret.

Lady Olivia was with Andre; their carriage came first, and they climbed inside. The next one was for Aislinn and Rose. As they left the ball, Aislinn asked, "What do you think of your first ball in London?"

"It was so exciting," Rose replied dutifully.

"I don't think you had very good luck finding suitors tonight," Aislinn added, raising her eyebrows and adjusting her position on the carriage's seat.

"It was just the slippers' fault, mother." Rose shrugged and turned her gaze to the dark streets. The first ball was over. Now, she would have to keep up her charade for the rest of the season to keep her promise to Arthur.

CHAPTER TWELVE

Arthur's Past

While the first party of the season was going on, Arthur and Ian had arrived at the townhouse. They noted that the house was empty, and Mattson, the butler, informed them that the ladies had gone to the ball.

"Ah, well, I guess Arthur can go with you to the servant's quarters. He's here for the rose competition. I'll go to my club for a couple of hours," Ian replied and headed back to his carriage.

Arthur stood there with his rose boxes, which he had packed for the competition. He carried a small bag containing his clothes. He didn't have anything suitable for the competition where he was expected to present his flowers.

Mattson glanced at him, took one of the boxes from him, and carried it.

Arthur remembered the house. He had been there when he was a small boy when Aislinn and her father had been imprisoned in Tower. He glanced around as Mattson, the butler, headed to the servants' quarters.

"I remember this house well, Mattson," Arthur commented when he walked after Mattson and climbed up the stairs to the small room on the third floor. "You took me in when we looked for the queen's assassins when Lord Ackley and Lady Aislinn were imprisoned. I'm glad I was able to help back then. I stayed here for a couple of nights."

"Yes, you were a smart young lad back then," Mattson replied and opened a door on the left. "This is your room now." Arthur stepped inside. It was a small room but clean. The bed was narrow, and there was a tiny window facing the side alley.

Arthur placed his box next to the one Mattson had carried. He explained, "I packed a couple of my best specimens of roses in these boxes for the Royal Society's competition. The duke saw me, then said I should come with him to London and present them myself instead of shipping them."

Mattson looked serious. "I know Rose has feelings for you. You should not encourage her. She is the duke's daughter."

"I know she is. But I love her, and she loves me." Arthur sighed. "I plan to make a lot of money with my roses, and I'm certain I can win this competition. My roses are the most beautiful you've ever seen. The winner will receive a prize of twenty-five thousand pounds. I can start my gardening business with that money. I'll get more customers when they see what beauties I can grow. When I have enough money to offer Rose the kind of living she's used to, then I will ask her hand."

Arthur's jaw tightened as he watched Mattson's face. He saw pity, then sadness. "Your love is not the problem," Mattson replied quietly. "The duke's daughter is from a different world, the world of noblemen. It's not our world. We are servants. You will break your heart if you keep believing you can have her. She will ruin her reputation if she is seen with you. Think what you're doing to both of you." After saying what he wanted to say, he sighed. "I know Aislinn loves you. She told me so. She wants to find out who your parents were and where you came from."

Arthur grinned. *Aislinn told Mattson she loves me!*

Mattson gestured to the bed, and Arthur sat down while Mattson sat on the only chair in the room. "Do you remember anything about your past?"

"I remember I was kept in a basement for a long time," Arthur replied, frowning. "It was dark. I was afraid of the rats that lived there. They bit me."

"Why were you in the basement? Were you alone?" Mattson asked.

"No, there was another boy too. He was dressed in fine silk clothes. He had fair hair up to his shoulders. They called him Darius." Arthur rubbed his chin, trying to remember more.

"What else do you remember?" Mattson asked. *A boy with fine clothes should not be with orphans. What is this?*

"Darius cried often. He wanted to go back to his mother and father. He told me he lived outside London in a big house. I think he was only four years old. I had been in the basement long before he arrived. I must have been six then," Arthur said.

"Did you hear his last name?" Mattson asked.

"No, I don't think so. I don't recall," Arthur replied and shook his head.

"What were you wearing?"

"I remember my shoes were too small. They were light blue with golden buttons. They might have been the correct size earlier, but my feet had grown. I had dark blue velvet breeches and a white shirt, which was dirty and had holes. I had rolled my jacket under my head as a pillow. It was of the same material as the breeches."

"How long were you there in that basement?" Mattson asked and leaned forward. This was not what he expected to hear from Arthur. He was not describing the clothes or the living of the middle or lower classes. He had been imprisoned!

"I don't know. For a long time. Weeks, months maybe."

"What happened to Darius?"

"One day, one of the men who kept us there took Darius and left me alone in the basement. I didn't see Darius after that. I was alone. One evening, the man forgot to lock the door, and I sneaked out. No one saw me leaving. I ran away as fast as I could and did not pay attention to where I went, just as long as it was away from that basement. When I got tired of running, I found a park, stayed overnight, and slept on the bench. Then I met the guys you saw me with when we met the first time: the group of orphan boys. I joined them, and they helped me to adjust to living on the streets."

Mattson had taken a notebook from his pocket and wrote a few lines. Then he asked, "What kind of buttons did you have on your clothes?"

Arthur frowned and turned his eyes to the ceiling as if trying to recall. "They had a flower in them. I remember I always thought they looked girlish. Why would boy's clothes have buttons with flowers." He smiled and added, "Now, since I discovered that I love gardening and roses, it seems fitting."

Flowers in buttons. It sounds like someone had hand-made them for those clothes, a special order, I would guess. So, I have two clues now: the buttons and the boy called Darius.

"What do you remember about Darius?" Mattson asked. "You were with him for a while. Did he tell you anything else about his family or his home?"

"Darius... I have not thought about him for a long time. He told me how he had ended up in that place. He had been playing outside with his nanny. Then someone had called his nanny, and he had been alone for a while, and a man approached and grabbed him and took him away. He had struggled and cried, but the man put a smelly cloth over his mouth, and he passed out. He woke up in that basement with me."

Darius was kidnapped! A big house with a nanny. His parents had money. A ransom perhaps, Mattson thought and wrote it down.

"Why were you in the basement?" Mattson asked.

Arthur shook his head. "I don't recall."

"What is the first memory you have?" Mattson inquired.

Arthur sighed. "A woman smiling at me. She was beautiful with blond hair. She had a necklace with shiny stones: green and red. I remember playing with the stones, and she laughed and said I might break it if I pull too hard."

That doesn't sound like a lower or working-class woman, either. Shiny stones could be jewels, Mattson thought. *It still does not mean he is noble*, he reminded himself. He wrote down the description of the necklace and the woman.

"What else?" Mattson turned his eyes on Arthur.

Arthur looked away to the window. *What else?* He raked his fingers through his hair. He had not tried to remember his past since he had been safe in Duke Manchester's estate. He had let the past be past.

"I recall a big white building. I don't know what it was. I remember a room with a large golden chandelier. I don't know whose house it was. I remember I rode with a small pony. Someone instructed me how to sit on the saddle. There was a lake near that building with white swans and lily pads. "

He is describing a noble home, Mattson thought. He wrote down everything Arthur had said.

"Can you describe any persons there? Or the men who kept you in the basement?" Mattson asked.

"The men who kept me in the basement were big and shaggy. They had black hair and dirty clothes, and their hands were filthy. They hit me if I cried. I got water to drink, a slice of bread, and a bowl of soup to eat most of the day. One of them was called Simon. I think he was the boss."

Simon. I could take this information to Scotland Yard and ask if they know anyone called Simon who leads a gang in London, Mattson thought, but then he realized Duke Ian would get better results with the police. He was not a servant but an aristocrat. *I should tell him about Arthur,* he thought.

"Okay, this is enough today. If you remember anything else, then let me know. Get some sleep."

"Good night, Mattson," Arthur said.

"Good night, Arthur," Mattson replied.

When Aislinn and Rose returned from the ball, Mattson mentioned that Duke had arrived and was in his club now. Aislinn's face brightened, and she replied, "I will retire now. He'll find me in my room. Thank you, Mattson." Rose followed her mother upstairs.

Mattson nodded. He didn't mention anything about Arthur.

He sat in the hallway and waited for Duke Ian to return.

He came back in an hour. When he saw Mattson waiting for him, he asked, "What is it? Is something wrong?"

"No, nothing. The ladies are back, and the duchess wanted to let you know she is in her room." He hesitated and Ian saw it and asked, "What else?"

"Can I talk to you privately in the library?" Mattson asked and gestured to the room on the other end of the hallway.

"Certainly." Ian walked there and sat down. He gestured for Mattson to sit too.

"What is it you want to talk about?" Ian asked.

Mattson took out his notes and said, "I've found something peculiar in Arthur's past."

Ian leaned forward. "What is it?"

"He is not an orphan. He might be a child of an aristocrat." He explained what Arthur had told him.

"That is interesting," Ian said. "We should take that information to Scotland Yard as you suggested. They might know more about him and this Darius he remembered."

"I think they would take you more seriously," Mattson added. "If a servant goes there, they might put all that information in a pile and forget about it. Arthur saved your wife and her father's lives. You owe him."

"I don't need to be reminded of that. I know it very well," Ian snapped. "I will take that information to the police, and you'll accompany me. You heard the story, so you can answer if they have more questions. We'll go tomorrow after breakfast."

"Thank you, sir," Mattson replied and gave a rare smile. "I've always liked Arthur. He was a good boy when he was an orphan."

Duke Ian nodded. "Yes, he was." He recalled how calmly Arthur had shown him the place where the Indian servants had met and how he had explained where they had sat. That was the clue that led to the arrest of the queen's assassins.

Everyone owes him, Ian thought. *The queen, me, Aislinn, and her father.*

CHAPTER THIRTEEN

Ian and Aislinn

Duke Ian stayed behind and walked to the side table to have another drink of whiskey. *What an interesting evening this is*, he thought. *Mattson revealed a secret that had been hidden.* Duke walked to the window and stood there for a moment, thinking about the news and what to do. It was getting late, he realized, and he was still up. He had not even seen his wife since she returned from the ball, but he was not in the mood for a light chatting of dresses and dances.

Sighing, he sank into a comfortable velvet sofa by the window. He twirled the drink in his glass, deep in thought. He had never asked the orphan boy about his memories. He had taken him to live in his estate and schooled him. Arthur liked gardening, so he let him stay and learn more about the flowers, especially the roses he loved.

What if I was wrong? What if I should have asked him about his past and what he remembered? I never did that. I always assumed he

was a homeless street boy. However, I always knew he was smart and
observant. He learned fast from whatever books we put in front of him.

He glanced at the doorway when he heard light steps. It was his
wife, Aislinn.

"I waited for you to come upstairs," she said. She wore a thin, light
blue robe over her nightgown. She held out her hand, and Ian took it,
kissed it, and pulled her to sit next to him.

"I'm sorry. I was just thinking about the news I learned tonight,"
Ian replied and passionately kissed his wife.

"What news?" Aislinn asked, leaning back and facing her husband.

"About Arthur," Ian replied.

"What about him?" Aislinn replied, surprised, hands still around
Ian's neck.

"It seems he is more than just an orphan boy. He has memories of
something else," Ian replied. "He might have been kidnapped when he
was a child. He also remembers another boy in the same place. A boy
named Darius with fine clothes. He also told Mattson that he wore
clothes with special flower buttons."

Aislinn leaned back. "That *is* some news!" She tilted her head and
asked, "How do you plan to find out who he is?"

Ian's eyes were on the drink he swirled on his hand when he replied,
"I talked with Mattson earlier tonight. We decided it would be better
to go to Scotland Yard and ask for their help with this case. They might
have kidnapping cases from back then, about fifteen years ago or so.
We don't know Arthur's birthday, or when he was born, so we can ask
approximate years when he might have been taken." He glanced at his
wife and added, "I think I should go with Mattson there tomorrow.
They will take me more seriously than just Mattson asking about this."

"I think you're right," Aislinn replied. "Also, I think I know someone else in the social circles who can help, someone who knows all the gossip of past years."

"Who is that?"

"Lady Olivia, of course. She's been in London for decades now. If she does not know all the society gossip, then she knows someone who does. I'm sure I'll get something out of her if I ask," Aislinn said, determined to help.

Ian nodded. "Yes, you're correct. She knows the families. She might recognize that crests with flowers. Can you ask her tomorrow? Perhaps we can then compare our notes after?"

"Yes, of course. I'll ask her to have tea with me." Aislinn kissed Ian and leaned back. "Please, don't tell Rose. She had a terrible evening. She doesn't need anything else to think about now."

"What do you mean with terrible?" Ian's eyebrow rose.

"She was so clumsy on the floor." Aislinn knitted her eyebrows. "First, everything went smoothly, and she danced so lovely with Andre, but then the next dance was a catastrophe. She tripped on her long train and stomped on her dance partner's foot. That was Viscount Smythe, and he pushed some other pairs on the floor. It was so embarrassing."

Ian tried not to smile.

Aislinn saw the twitch of her mouth, and she said, "Don't you dare smile! We are talking about our daughter and her first ball!"

Ian tried to keep her face solemn, which was hard. "What happened next?"

Aislinn sighed. "She tripped, and her cake flew on the next suitor's shirt!"

Now, Ian couldn't help but laugh.

Aislinn frowned at him. "Rose didn't get any more suitors after that, and that's nothing to laugh about!"

"I'm sure she didn't. But it was funny, wasn't it?" Ian laughed, and Aislinn had a hard time keeping her face angry.

She started laughing too. "Yes, I guess it was funny," she admitted wiping tears of laughter from her eyes.

"I would pay a handsome sum of money to see the faces of those two Rose's suitors," Ian added.

"They were not pleased, I can tell you that," Aislinn replied.

"Do you think Rose was nervous?" Ian asked.

"I'm not sure. She looked pensive when we went to the ball. At first, everything looked normal, but then her evening turned into a disaster. Perhaps, she was nervous. She has never been to London and attended a ball. It can be frightening with all the families and suitors assessing you," Aislinn admitted.

"Was that how you felt at your first ball?" Ian asked, his eyes twinkling. That was how they had met, at a ball in London.

Aislinn smiled. "No, I was excited! And then I met you!"

Ian leaned toward her and kissed her. "And we've been together ever since. I love you, my dear Aislinn."

"I love you too, Ian."

"Let's go upstairs. It's getting late, and we have a lot to do tomorrow." Ian rose and pulled Aislinn up. They walked together to the hallway and headed upstairs.

CHAPTER FOURTEEN

At Scotland Yard

Duke Ian dressed in his finest grey wool suit with a grey silk vest and a tie. He had a quick breakfast around seven o'clock because he didn't want to stay and chat with his daughter or wife. He took his wool hat from Mattson in the hallway, and they were ready to go. The other staff knew Mattson and the duke would be gone for an hour or so. Mattson had left a note for Arthur to let him know to wait for their return and not to go anywhere.

Arthur needed a new outfit for the rose competition, but that would have to wait until their return.

The carriage was ready, and when Ian stepped inside, Mattson went to the front seat with the driver, and they rode away. They headed to the New Scotland Yard building, which was recently opened in 1890 on the Thames Embankment. Duke Ian knew that Scotland Yard kept extensive files on all known criminals in the country and had a special branch of police who guarded the royalty and statesmen. That was why he was sure they would find some clues about Arthur's past there. They had to know about kidnappings back in the days of the old Scotland Yard. He was sure that Scotland Yard would have been informed if any noble family had lost or had their child kidnapped. The duke had visited there only once when he had to tell his part of the Queen's assassination and how he found out who the real culprits were.

When the carriage arrived at the headquarters of London's famous police force, Ian straightened in his seat and glanced through the window outside. It was early, so he hoped Scotland Yard investigators would not be too busy that time of day.

Duke Ian thought about the past and how Arthur helped save Aislinn and Lord Ackley. *If I can do anything now to help Arthur, I must do it*, Ian thought, determined. *I owe him my wife's life and my happiness.*

When the carriage stopped in front of the massive building. Mattson came and opened the door for Ian. He stepped outside and viewed the doorway. "Let's go," he said to Mattson, and they entered the building together. A faint cigar scent lingered in the air when they entered the lobby, where a police officer was taking down the names of the visitors and requesting the reason for their visit. No one was before the duke and Mattson, so they were greeted immediately.

After further discussion, Duke Ian and Mattson were taken to see Superintendent Edgar Allender. He was a young fellow, not more than twenty-five, tall and thin, and his hair was dark. His eyes were sharp and blue, meeting a glance squarely. He wore a wrinkled suit with a dark brown vest. A pipe was on the corner of his desk with piles of papers and files, which were cases he was involved in or browsing through.

Superintendent Edgar Allender brushed his hair with his hand when he got up, making sure he looked presentable in front of the duke. He had a habit of rubbing his head when thinking, so his hair was usually messed up.

"Please, sit down, Duke Manchester," Superintendent Allender said, pointing at the chairs in front of his large writing desk. Ian and Mattson sat down.

Superintendent Edgar Allender tidied his paper stacks, then turned his sharp eyes on the duke and asked, "What was it that you wanted to see me for this morning, Duke Manchester?"

"I have a case of an orphan boy," Ian started. Then he explained what he knew about Arthur, and Mattson completed his descriptions of Arthur and the other boy called Darren and the details of their clothes and flower buttons.

"Did he describe the other boy?" Superintendent Allender asked, pulling out a notepad, taking a pen in his hand and making some notes while he listened to the story.

"Yes, he was fair-haired and dressed in fine silk clothes. His hair was up to his shoulders," Mattson replied.

"What does Arthur look like? Or what did he look like when he was a child?" the superintendent continued asking, scribbling on a paper in front of him.

"Arthur is fair-haired and blue-eyed," Mattson replied.

"And why are you here?" Superintendent Allender asked, leaning back on his chair and facing the duke and Mattson.

"I hoped to find some clues if there were kidnapping cases back when Arthur was a young boy. That would be about twenty years ago or so. In addition, if you have a file of another boy kidnapped around the same time whose name was Darius," Ian said calmly.

Superintendent Edgar Allender stayed still for a long time. "Wait here for a moment," he said and got up and walked out of his room.

Ian heard his steps in the hallway and then some sounds of distant discussion. The sound of two sets of footsteps came closer, and the inspector arrived with a heavyset elderly man with a large white mustache, a black suit, and a green vest. "This is Inspector Farr." Farr had a file under his arm.

The duke shook hands with Farr, who took a seat on the other side of the table next to Superintendent Allender. Farr started the conversation. "I was the lead investigator in cases of missing or abducted noble children in the old Scotland Yard. If you can repeat the details of the boys, I might be able to help you."

Ian glanced at Mattson and nodded, and Mattson explained again what he had heard from Arthur.

Farr opened the file he had. He handed over a painting of a young boy, perhaps age four or five. He had long fair hair and was dressed in a blue silk shirt and knee-length pants. "This is Darius Fitzgerald, a young lord. He was taken from his home outside, and the nanny was suspected back then. She didn't know where the young lord had gone or what had happened to him. Later, the family received a blackmail letter asking for five hundred pounds for the boy, and if the family didn't pay, they would kill the boy." He opened a small letter, pulled out a blond lock of hair, showed it to Ian and Mattson, and added, "The kidnappers sent this lock of hair to prove they had captured the boy."

"So, Arthur's story was true!" Ian said.

"Yes, it seems so," Farr replied. "We never found out where they kept the stolen children. We didn't know about this basement your Arthur mentioned. That's a new clue."

"What happened to Darius?" Ian asked. "Could he tell us more about the kidnappers?"

Farr shook his head. "No, they made sure he couldn't tell anyone anything. They returned him home, but they had blinded him. He kept crying and crying, and he never recovered from the abduction. I think his family was beside themselves when they got him back blind, and they tried to do everything for him, but his mind was gone. He never spoke again after that. His family took him to a private sanitarium. I think he is still there. He was blinded because the kidnappers knew he could identify them."

"Arthur escaped. He didn't remember where he lived, so he stayed in London," Mattson said.

"That probably saved his life," Farr said grimly. "If the kidnappers went back to his home to look for him, they couldn't find him. Arthur can still identify those men."

"He is a grown man now," Ian added. "He has lived at my estate all his life since I found him, and he has not been back to London."

"That's good. He could still be in danger," Farr said. He opened his file again and took out a list of families with missing children. He browsed the list, following the missing children's names and details, and then stopped at a familiar name and tapped the paper with his finger. "Arthur Stanley. He went missing when he was about four years old. The kidnappers sent several letters and demands to his family, asking for different amounts. The family was very wealthy, and the kidnappers decided to ask for more money, thus keeping Arthur for a long time as their prisoner."

"What is the crest of the Stanleys?" Ian asked.

"A flower crest with a lion and a unicorn," Farr replied.

"A flower matches what Arthur remembered," Ian said.

"Yes, here is a painting of Arthur when he was about three, four years old," Farr said, digging out an old painting of a child.

Ian reached and grabbed the painting eagerly. A blond-haired boy with serious eyes. He wore a dark blue uniform with flower buttons, similar to what Arthur had described. Mattson leaned and viewed the painting too. "It's Arthur!" he said, wiping a tear from his eye. "He looked so serious when we met him the first time. He was not like the other orphan boys. He paid attention to details. He was smart."

Farr rubbed his chin. "We should proceed carefully. First, I would like to take Arthur to Stanley's stately estate. It's just outside London. He might remember it or perhaps not. He was very young when he was taken."

"I'd like to join you," Ian said.

Farr nodded. "That's fine."

"Do Stanley's have more children than Arthur?" Ian asked.

"He has a sister who was not yet born when Arthur was taken," Farr said, reading from his notes. "His mother was devastated, as was his father, because the title goes to the male heir, and Arthur was their only heir."

Ian nodded. "It would be better not to mention anything about that to Arthur yet. We might be wrong. I don't want to give him false hopes of finding his family."

Both the inspector and the superintendent nodded in agreement. "Of course. We need to be careful. If you don't mind, I would like to go to Stanley's estate as soon as possible."

"We can go there today afternoon. We need to drop off Arthur's roses to the competition, and after that, we are at your disposal," Ian replied.

"What is that competition?" Farr asked.

"It's a gardening competition arranged by the Royal Society," Ian replied. "Arthur is especially gifted in gardening and growing roses. He has several rose plants with him, which he has entered in the competition."

"Ah, the plants are in his genes, I guess. His father is a famous botanist and has developed several important plant-based medicines," Farr said.

Ian glanced at Mattson. "Yes, that would explain Arthur's skills in gardening and developing new roses."

Ian stood up, shook hands with the two police officers, and said, "Could you meet Arthur and me this afternoon around three at the Royal Society? We could go to see Stanley's estate after that."

"Yes, that would be my pleasure," Farr replied.

When Ian walked out of the building, he said, "We must get Arthur better clothes. Can you take him to my tailor and ask him if he has anything ready that would fit Arthur?"

"Yes, I will take care of that," Mattson replied and opened the carriage door for Ian. He closed the door, then stepped up to sit next to the driver.

Chapter Fifteen

Arthur

The duke's tailor was located at Regent Street next to the shoe and hat stores for gentlemen. Mattson took Arthur to meet the tailor, Mr. Squids, who was surprised to see the young man instead of the duke himself, but when Mattson gave the tailor the duke's orders to charge him, Mr. Squids was most pleased. First, he frowned because he was not sure if he could get anything ready so fast, but when he measured Arthur, he smiled and said, "We have a suit for him ready. It's only because one gentleman got into financing problems, and we had to keep the suit. He's about the same size as this young man. Let me get a shirt first, and then you can try on the suit."

The shirt was a thin white cotton shirt. As Arthur put it on behind a divider, Mr. Squid went to get the suit. It was a formal grey suit. Nothing too fancy but perfect for a respectable gentleman. He also got a grey hat and a tie with thin stripes.

After Arthur was dressed, he viewed himself in the mirror. He looked like a young gentleman except for his boots. They were worn brown leather boots, and he had used them while gardening for a couple of years. "We need to go to the shoe store next," Mattson commented, frowning.

"No, let me go and fetch a pair of boots from there," Mr. Squids said and hurried outside, and in a few minutes, he returned to the store with a pair of black boots in his hands. "These should be a perfect size," he muttered and handed them to Arthur, who pulled them on.

"Yes, they are." He walked around trying them out. They were stiffer than his previous ones but good quality leather. *They will last many years,* he thought, pleased.

As they had finished shopping, Mattson said, "Please, charge the duke's account for all of this. I will have to take him to a barbershop next."

Mr. Squids was pleased and hopped ahead to open the door. He was excited to have the duke's ward as his newest customer. He didn't believe a word of what Mattson had said, that Arthur was only a servant.

No, this man is a nobleman, Mr. Squids thought as he watched Arthur walk away. He was no servant. His posture and walk were like a man who knew who he was and what he wanted in life. *No lower-class man walks like that,* he thought.

While Mattson and Arthur were shopping, Aislinn went to have tea and biscuits with Lady Olivia in their townhouse. She was pleased to find Lady Olivia at home. She wore a light blue morning dress, and her hair was curled and gathered on top of her head and decorated with small blue flowers and pearls.

"How lovely to see you again so soon after the ball. I hope your daughter is not too disappointed in her first ball," Lady Olivia said and led her to the dining room. She instructed the maid to bring some tea with cookies and biscuits.

Aislinn sat down and smoothed her lavender dress with her hand. "I don't think Rose is sad or disappointed. It was her first appearance; anyone can have mishaps as she had. We must see that her slippers are not too slippery next time. She complained that they were too smooth, and she couldn't walk or dance with them."

The maid brought in a tray, and Lady Olivia waited for her to serve it. When the maid left, she asked, "Did you have something else to ask?"

"Yes, in fact, I do have," Aislinn replied. "Do you remember any old incident, about twenty or so years ago, when a child had been kidnapped?"

"Do you mean a child of a member of our society?" Lady Olivia asked. Now she was curious.

"Yes, that's what I mean. Did someone abduct a child and ask for ransom?" Aislinn confirmed.

She took a long sip, peering over the edge of her porcelain cup, watching as Lady Olivia tried to jog her memory to remember the details of the past incidents involving kidnappings.

"Yes, I believe there was," Lady Olivia said slowly. "I remember a couple of cases. One was a young lord who got lost, and the other was a family with a large estate outside London. I think it was an earl who had lost his only heir."

"Do you remember any details?" Aislinn asked, holding her breath.

"I think the lord's son was returned, but he had gone insane. The other one never came back." Lady Olivia stared at the fireplace. "It was so sad. The lord was devastated when his son returned and was mutilated and insane. Everyone believed the other boy would be returned too, but he never was. The earl had paid the ransom, but he didn't get his son back. The family mourned for months."

Aislinn agreed. So sad for the boy. However, the other boy had not been found, and there was a chance that Arthur was the lost son of an earl.

Lady Olivia lifted the teacup. While sipping her tea, she asked, "Why do you ask about such old history?"

"We might know where the other boy is," Aislinn said. "Ian might have rescued him when he was a child." Then she told the story to Lady Olivia, who listened to her with her eyes widening.

"That's excellent news!" Lady Olivia replied. "Astonishing."

"Ian is now at Scotland Yard to find out the identity of the abducted boys," Aislinn replied.

"Please, tell me when you know more. This is a great story to tell at the next ball," Lady Olivia said.

"You'll have to wait for the confirmation. Besides, I don't know if Scotland Yard wants to investigate the abductions before saying anything to the public. If I guess right, the criminals are still out there, and we don't want to put this young man in any danger," Aislinn warned Lady Olivia, who nodded.

CHAPTER SIXTEEN

Rose

Rose woke up the next morning after the ball. She stretched in her bed and didn't bother to hurry downstairs. Maid Lillian knocked on the door around ten a.m. and peeked inside. She knew Rose must be tired after dancing, but it was almost midday, and she should get up now.

Lillian was still a good-looking woman about fifteen years older than Rose. She had been a teenager when she started to work at Ackley's mansion. Now she was about to marry a pastor and was positively radiating happiness. She had worked for Aislinn for many years and saw Rose grow up. She curtsied when she entered the room and walked to pull the curtains away from the windows. "Good morning, miss." She returned to the bedside and said, "Would you like to have your breakfast here or downstairs?"

"I can come downstairs," Rose replied.

"Let me get you ready," Lillian replied. She took out a day dress with a light pink color and matching shoes and put them on top of the bed. She helped Rose into her dress, waited for her to sit by the dresser, and then started gently brushing her hair. "How was your night, Miss Rose?"

"Ghastly," Rose said. "I did not like anyone who came to ask me to dance except Andree. He was great!"

Lillian kept styling Rose's hair so that locks fell on her shoulders while she curled part at the back of her head and put pins with tiny beads on the bun.

"Why are you here helping me to get dressed and not helping my mother?" Rose asked. Lillian was usually always with Aislinn, not her.

"The duchess left early this morning to visit Lady Olivia. The duke also left with Mattson, so there wasn't much else for me to do," Lillian replied and finished styling Rose's hair. "How do you like your hair?"

"It looks wonderful," Rose nodded. "Why did my mother go to see Lady Olivia? We just saw her yesterday?" Rose didn't expect Lillian to know that, but she might have overheard something when her mother left the house. She was worried that her mother would discuss the balls and suitors with Lady Olivia, and she didn't want that.

"She had something important to ask Lady Olivia. It had something to do with a secret and is also why your father and Mattson left early," Lillian replied. She had not heard much but just bits and pieces.

"That sounds strange," Rose said. *A secret? And both her parents and Mattson left early because of it. What was going on?*

Rose was ready to go to have breakfast. She ran downstairs and went to the kitchen. She asked the cook if she could sit there and have toast with jam and some tea. She didn't want to eat alone in the dining room if no one else was home. The cook was happy to serve her there.

After breakfast, she wondered what she should do. She walked to the hallway and then to the library. She picked up a book and started reading it. A couple of hours went by, and then she heard noises from the front door. Her mother had come home. Rose put the book aside and rushed to the hallway.

"Hello, Rose," Aislinn said when she saw her daughter coming to greet her. Aislinn kissed Rose on the cheek and said, "How are you feeling this morning?"

"Great!" Rose replied. She hesitated, then asked, "Why did you go to see Lady Olivia?"

Aislinn frowned, then said, "Your father said not to tell you anything yet."

"Does it have something to do with me?" Rose asked.

"No, not directly, but knowing about it could be dangerous, or so your father believes," Aislinn replied cryptically.

At just that moment, Mattson and Arthur returned after their shopping trip.

Aislinn and Rose both turned and stared at the two men. They knew Mattson, but Arthur looked different in a gentleman's outfit. It seemed that the right clothes made the man. He seemed to be walking straighter and looked more assertive than ever before.

When Arthur saw Rose, he smiled brightly and said, "Hello, Miss Rose," and then greeted Aislinn more formally, "Duchess."

"Arthur? You're in London," Rose uttered, not believing her eyes.

"Yes, Duke Ian asked me to come and stay here while I participate in the rose competition," Arthur replied.

"You're staying here?" Rose asked.

"Yes, in the servant's quarters," Arthur confirmed.

Mattson interrupted. "We are in a hurry. We need to pick up his plants for the exhibition at the Royal Society, and we will meet Duke

Ian there." Mattson glanced at Aislinn, and they seemed to exchange some unsaid words.

Aislinn asked, "Mattson, could you come to the dining room? I want to speak with you. Arthur, you can pick up your plants while Mattson is with me."

Arthur nodded and left the room, and Mattson followed Aislinn. Rose was about to follow them, but Aislinn shook her head. "No, Rose. Wait for me at the library." She closed the door in front of Rose's nose.

"Tell me what happened at Scotland Yard," Aislinn asked Mattson, and he told Aislinn what they learned from the police.

"So, Arthur may be a child of a nobleman," Aislinn said quietly. "How strange. I always thought he was clever, and he learned fast."

"His father could be a famous botanist," Mattson added.

"That explains Arthur's interest in flowers," Aislinn said. "What happens next?"

"We'll meet Inspector Farr at the Royal Society, then we'll go to Stanley's estate to see if Arthur remembers it." Mattson glanced at his watch on a chain in his vest pocket and said, "I'm afraid we have to go now. The duke is waiting for us there."

"I'm coming too," Aislinn said determinedly. She wanted to see the plants in the competition and follow up on what happened next.

"Very well. I will let the driver know, and we'll take two carriages. One for you and one for Arthur and his plants," Mattson replied. He did not want to argue with the duchess.

"I will take Rose with me. She would love to see the different roses at the Royal Society," Aislinn added. She also knew Rose would like to see how Arthur's roses compared with the other roses. She headed to the library and saw Rose by the window. "We're going to the Royal Society. Are you ready?"

"Yes! Thank you, mother," Rose flew to hug her mother and said, "I will just grab my bonnet, my purse, and my gloves and I'm ready." She ran upstairs and returned with her bonnet on her head, her purse in her hand, and she pulled her gloves onto her hands while descending.

Aislinn was ready because she had her bonnet and gloves downstairs after visiting Lady Olivia. She wondered if Lady Olivia had yet figured out who the kidnapped boy was. *Lady Olivia will hear more later*, Aislinn decided. *We'll see how everything goes at Stanley's estate.*

CHAPTER SEVENTEEN

At the Royal Society

When Aislinn stepped outside, a servant approached the front door. "I have a message from Lady Olivia Ackley to Duchess Manchester." He bowed and handed the note to Mattson, who took it and then turned and gave it to Aislinn. Lady Olivia's servant waited for an answer and stood patiently while Aislinn viewed the note.

Aislinn glanced at the note and then told the servant, "Tell Lady Olivia that I will meet her at the Royal Society with Rose."

The servant nodded and left.

This is going to be interesting, Aislinn thought and put the note in her purse. *Lady Olivia has found something relevant and said she will meet me at the Royal Society's flower contest. She might have found out who Arthur is and wants to tell me that, but I already know.*

Aislinn sat in her carriage next to Rose in deep thought. Rose nudged her mother with her elbow and asked, "What's going on? You have been so quiet since reading Aunt Olivia's note."

Their carriage drove first, and Mattson was in the second one with Arthur and his plants. Mattson was also pensive as he had not told Arthur anything he had learned at Scotland Yard. He did not want the young man to be anxious or upset. *What if he meets his biological father today? Will Arthur recognize him? Will Arthur's biological father recognize him? What will it be like to find he has a family after all these years? And what will it be like to meet your son after so long?* Mattson had no idea.

Arthur was also in deep thought. In his mind, he went through the details of his roses, their best qualities, and why they should win the competition. He knew that the plants would be judged by esteemed authorities in botany and gardening and would be assessed on various criteria ranging from the overall presentation, the symmetry of the flower and petals, disease resistance, durability, and the presence of fragrance. He sighed. Now, he was not sure if he was ready for the contest. He knew he had done his best, but he was still a servant. Many noblemen would also compete and would not look kindly on a lowlife like him. Duke Ian had been nice to dress him up to better match the other competitors, but Arthur knew that he lacked in knowledge and behavior of those who had lived a life of luxury. He stared outside but didn't pay attention to any of the views.

Arthur straightened his shoulders and blinked when the carriage finally turned in front of a large greenhouse and parked. *Now we are here*, he thought. He glanced at his plants carefully packed in separate boxes and hoped they had traveled well in the containers.

Mattson said, "Duke Ian will wait for us somewhere around the main building behind the greenhouse. He wants us to go and meet him there after you have set up your presentation. I assume you know where you go and place your roses?"

Arthur nodded. Clearing his throat, he replied, "Yes, I received the instructions in the letter where they informed me that my roses were accepted to the contest, sir."

The older man said, "Good, I will leave you to take care of them, and we'll meet you by the main building later."

Mattson got out first and went to help the ladies in the next carriage leaving Arthur to take care of his plants.

CHAPTER EIGHTEEN

Arthur's Father

Duke Ian walked around the crowd to find the famous botanist, Frederick Stanley, Count of Warrendale. He saw the competition judges were wearing blue ribbons on their coat's lapels, so it was fairly easy to spot them. They walked slowly past the tables where the competitors had placed their plants according to the category they had enlisted: bouquets, a variety of flowers, or single plants like roses and tulips. The three judges walked one after another. Duke Ian recognized all of them and had exchanged a few words with them before.

Ian went after them, and when they took a break, he approached one of the judges, namely Frederick Stanley. "Excuse me, sir. I'm Duke Ian Manchester, and I have an urgent and private issue to discuss with you. If you could spare me a couple of minutes, I will explain the urgency."

Frederick Stanley was a stout and tall man. He wore no lace on his collar like many aristocrats, but Duke Ian immediately noticed the expensive weave of his shirt and waistcoat with the famous flower buttons. His wheat-colored hair had a few grey highlights and was pulled into a ponytail at the back of his head. Lastly, Ian looked at Stanley's face and recognized the familiar nose, eyes, and eyebrows matching Arthur's. Stanley's face might have been handsome if he smiled, but it seemed like a deep sorrow had etched his face into a permanent gloomy look.

"I have twenty minutes before the competition starts," Stanley replied, looking curious. "However, if you plan to influence the results of the competition, then let me assure you that it won't work. I will judge based on the rules we have on this competition and not based on the relationship of the competitor or how wealthy his family is." He looked stern when he said the last part warning Ian not to meddle with the competition results.

Ian shook his head and smiled. "No, absolutely not. I have a family issue that I would like to discuss with you. Could we go over there, so we can have a discreet conversation and privacy?" He gestured with his hand to the left side of the main building, where he had seen a pathway leading to the back of the house. "I think you will understand why I need to get you away from the crowd when you hear my business."

Stanley frowned but was also curious. It was not usual for a well-known and respected aristocrat like Duke Ian to approach and ask for a private conversation. "Very well, like I said, we don't start for twenty minutes, so that is all the time I can give you, Duke Manchester."

Ian nodded. "Please, call me Ian. I don't like titles so much, and my topic is of personal interest to me. Please, follow me." He started walking to the path he had pointed out, and Frederick Stanley followed him.

When they had walked a bit further away from the crowd, Ian stopped, checked that no one was in hearing distance, and turned to Stanley. "It's about your son, Arthur."

Stanley looked angry at first and then suspicious. "My son is dead. There is no need to continue this discussion." He was about to turn away when Ian grabbed his arm, locked his eyes on Stanley, and said quietly, "He is not dead. He will be here soon." He saw the disbelief in Stanley's eyes and added, "Inspector Farr of the Scotland Yard will be here soon, too, and if you don't believe me, you will believe him."

Stanley took a deep breath, opened his mouth, and closed it again as if he was unsure what to say. "How? Where?"

Ian said, "Let us walk forward. I don't want to attract any attention. Someone might still be watching your family."

Stanley nodded and followed Ian.

Ian started his story. "Arthur was just a child when I met him first. He saved the life of my wife and her father. He was smart and brave even when he was a child. He stayed with me at my estate and studied with my daughter Rose when she had a governess. When Rose left for a boarding school, Arthur expressed his wish to learn more about flowers and gardening, and I was happy to grant his wish. He is a bright young man and a talented gardener. I must tell you that he is a participant in this contest you have here. I won't tell you who he is until the contest is over so that you will not be affected in your judgment. I will tell you this now because you might recognize him. I immediately noticed a familiar forehead, nose, eyebrows, and eyes when I saw you. His hair color is darker than yours, though."

Frederick Stanley asked, "Why he didn't come home?"

"He didn't know he had a home or didn't remember where it was. He was just a child back then. I only learned about his memories recently. I contacted Scotland Yard, and they had information about the old kidnapping cases. Inspector Farr helped me to discover who Arthur is or was."

"How can you be sure he is my son?" Frederick Stanley asked. "Anyone can claim they are him, and they could be frauds."

"First of all, he does not claim to be your son. He does not know anything about you," Ian replied and added, "I found you based on the information I received from the Scotland Yard and what Arthur remembered." Then Ian explained Arthur's memories of a basement or a cellar where he had been kept with another child called Darius. That alerted Stanley, who said, "Darius was kidnapped about the same time as my son. He was returned but blinded. He never recovered." Stanley sniffed and added, "I paid a handsome ransom to get him back. I hoped for a new ransom when Arthur didn't come back home, but no one contacted me. I suspected they had killed my son. I never thought he had escaped."

"Arthur escaped the kidnappers and lived on the streets. That's why they never contacted you again." They walked side by side forward, and Ian said, "Arthur remembered his clothes that day. He remembers a large house and a nanny."

Frederick Stanley nodded. "His home."

"I never told Arthur about you or your estate. I will meet Inspector Farr here, and we hope to visit your estate after the competition. Arthur will be with us. If you don't mind, I think it will be interesting to see if he remembers the place," Ian replied.

"I will come with you," Stanley replied. He took out his pocket watch and said, "I have to excuse myself now. The competition starts in a few minutes."

Ian said, "Of course. Can we meet here after the competition? I will find Inspector Farr, and we'll wait for you here."

"That sounds good," Frederick Stanley replied. When he walked away, his steps had a new spring in them, as if he had a new reason to live.

CHAPTER NINETEEN

The Conversation

Duke Ian looked around to find his wife and daughter and finally saw them walking toward the main building's direction. He went to greet them and kissed his wife on the cheek. "Is Mattson with Arthur?"

Aislinn nodded. "Yes, he helped Arthur to carry his plants to the exhibition table."

"Good, we can go there to see how his roses succeed," Ian replied and offered his arm to Aislinn and Rose. They moved along the pathway between the exhibition tables, and Aislinn kept her eyes on the women. She was looking for Lady Olivia.

Ian noticed this and asked, "Who are you looking for?"

"Olivia said she would be here. She said she had some news, or rather rumors, I guess," Aislinn replied. Then she tapped his arm and said, "She's over there. Let's go to talk to her." She brushed past the slow-walking couples and caught Lady Olivia by the bouquet exhibition.

Lady Olivia wore a dark red dress that emphasized her narrow waist and bosom. Her flower-decorated hat was tipped on a jaunty angle and had a tiny hand fan on her right hand. She turned around just when Aislinn was close by and looked pleased to see them. She air-kissed Aislinn and Rose, and Ian nodded to her. Because they were relatives, they didn't greet each other formally.

"I have some news," Lady Olivia started, swiveling her head around to see if anyone was listening. "Perhaps, we could go over there," she added as she saw a tall oak tree close by and gestured at it. They went there, and Lady Olivia fanned her face and said, "Several children were taken from their homes about ten to fifteen years ago. The children were of different ages, but mostly young children. Some were boys, and a couple were girls. Most of them were returned to their families after the families paid a hefty ransom to the kidnappers."

Ian interrupted. "How do you know all this?"

Lady Olivia glanced at him, assessing his stern face before replying. "This morning, after talking to Aislinn, I went to see an old gossiper, Countess Bartleton. She knows all the gossip and rumors of the past twenty years. There is no gossip she has not heard. She is the one person who knows all the high society families and their members and all the rumors about them."

"What did she tell you?" Aislinn asked curiously and twirled her fan in her hand.

"The kidnappers were never found. The families suspected it had to be either a servant or a member of the high society who was behind all this. One rumor suggested that someone needed money to cover up his gaming debts and had created this kidnapping plot to get access to more money. However, the one child, Darius, who was blinded, knew the kidnappers. The rumor was back then that he could identify the kidnapper, so he was blinded. It was also rumored that another child had escaped from the kidnappers but was never found," Lady Olivia said and viewed her audience. She saw keen interest in their faces.

Ian said, "That's about what we found out at Scotland Yard. Do you know who the society suspected was the gambler behind all this?"

Lady Olivia frowned. "Harold Smythe, the Earl of Chesterton."

"Because of his sudden flux of money," Ian replied. "I remember that. He owed me some money too, quite a lot if I remember correctly, and suddenly he paid it all. He explained he had gotten lucky in card games, which I didn't believe because he was a lousy player."

Rose's eyes widened when she heard the name. His son, Viscount Gerald Smythe, was the one who had asked her to dance at the ball! She recalled his thick, wavy blond hair, double chin, potbelly, and small eyes, which looked at her as if he hated her and wanted to punish her after the fall on the dancefloor. "I met his son," Rose said quietly. The others turned to face her. "At the ball," Aislinn said. "I remember that now. Your dance performance was quite exquisite."

Rose nodded. "Yes, I stumbled, and he fell on the floor."

Ian laughed out loud. "That's my girl! I wish I had seen it."

Rose tried to hide her smile.

Aislinn looked sternly at her husband and said, "Don't encourage her. She was not behaving like a lady."

Rose rolled her eyes. She didn't care for that man or any other one. The only one she cared about was Arthur.

Ian nodded to the path where they had left and said, "That foxy-looking man is Inspector Farr. I promised to meet him here. We can meet again by Arthur's exhibition table." He walked away to greet the inspector and told him the rumors Lady Olivia had heard.

CHAPTER TWENTY

The Flower Competition

Arthur had placed her three rose plants on the table with his participation number on the corner so the judges would know whom they were assessing.

He reconsidered his choices of rose plants. Were they good enough? He glanced around at the tables next to him, and he had to admit the competitors had excellent plants too. Arthur's choices were his Sunrise Rose, which had hints of orange on the yellow petals, Ackley's Dream, which was a classic white rose with a hint of pink inside, and his third choice was the Magnificent Rose, which was a dark red rose. He hoped the judges would see how special his roses were and notice the different fragrances. He knew those were the criteria on which the roses were supposed to be assessed, but he also knew that when you smell and view dozens of roses on the same day, you will lose the sense of smell and get tired. Also, he suspected that his background as a gardener was not good enough to win this competition, although that was his dream.

He kept his eyes on the three judges as they walked slowly, exchanged words with the competitors, made notes on each table, smelled and examined the plants and the flowers, counted the petals, and measured the size of the flowers. It was a painstakingly slow process. Arthur wished he had been on one of the first tables so that his roses would have received the attention they deserved.

Mattson stood next to him and said, "You'll be just fine. Don't worry."

Arthur turned his eyes to him and said, "What if the roses are not good enough? What would I do then? I love Rose."

"I know you do. I'm sure you'll find a way to be with her," Mattson replied cryptically and then quickly added, "Duke Ian is approaching with another gentleman."

Arthur turned his eyes to the approaching people, his eyes searching the crowd to find a familiar face. The duke was a couple of tables away and walking toward him. Arthur straightened his back and watched him approach. The other man was a stranger to him.

Duke Ian came to stand next to Arthur and said, "Good afternoon, Arthur. Let me introduce you to Inspector Farr. He's from the Scotland Yard."

Arthur extended his hand, and Inspector Farr shook it with a tight grip. "I am very pleased to meet you, Arthur," he said, studying the young man's face. He nodded to Duke Ian and said, "You're right. I can see the resemblance."

Resemblance? What are they talking about? Arthur wondered, but he didn't have time to ask because the judges were at his table now.

They viewed the plants, did the same measurements, checked the number of petals and the fragrance of each rose and wrote notes. Arthur answered their questions as well as he could. He relaxed when he was able to talk about his roses, and his words came out easily.

One of the judges, a tall man with light-colored hair, studied him with a curious look. Arthur was surprised when he saw tears coming to the judge's eyes. What was going on? The judge looked at Duke Ian and Inspector Farr and nodded, "It is him. I'm sure."

When the two other judges had left, the third judge extended his hand to Arthur and said, "It was a pleasure to meet you, Arthur. I will see you soon." Then he left and caught up with the other two judges. Arthur shook his head in surprise. "What did the judge mean?" He turned to Duke Ian and Inspector Farr, and they looked at him with smiles on their faces.

"Dear boy, we have some news for you, but let us wait for the results of your competition first before we tell you," Duke Ian said and patted Arthur on his back.

Then his eyes caught on Aislinn, Lady Olivia, and Rose, and he added, "Let's greet our ladies. They are coming to see your roses."

Arthur blushed. He had not expected Rose to be present. What if he lost?

It took another half an hour before the judges announced the competition winners.

Arthur tugged his shirt collar as if it had gotten too tight for him. He brushed his hair with his hand and faced the podium where the judges gathered. The crowd fell silent.

"The third prize goes to…" Arthur closed his eyes. He didn't even hear whom they announced. Same with the second one. One more prize left. "And the main prize goes to our first-time competitor, Arthur Smith, for his rose Magnificent Rose."

Arthur opened his eyes. He had won! He didn't even listen to the judges' arguments. He sighed and turned to face the group of people congratulating him. Rose squeezed his hands, Mattson patted his back, and so did the duke and the inspector. When he walked through the crowd to receive his prize, many unfamiliar faces congratulated him. He climbed on the podium to greet the judges. The rest of the reception was a blur.

The third judge, whose name he didn't know, stood by Arthur and beamed as if he had won. Duke Ian and the others had followed Arthur to the podium, and when the crowd started parting, Inspector Farr said, "We should go now." He turned to the third judge and asked, "Do you come with us?"

"Yes, of course," the third judge replied and then held out his hand to Arthur and said, "We were not officially introduced. My name is Frederick Stanley. I'm Count of Warrendale."

Arthur shook his hand and said, "Arthur Smith, at your service, sir."

"It's not Smith, dear boy," Duke Ian interrupted. "You'll soon know your real family name. That's the big news we have for you. Let us go now. The ladies will take their carriages, but we will go first with Inspector Farr and Frederick on my carriage, and you will join us."

Arthur nodded. He didn't know what to think.

Chapter Twenty-One

Arthur's Memories

It wasn't that easy to leave the exhibition area. Arthur received congratulations from so many passersby that he didn't even know how many hands he shook. Eventually, Duke Ian approached him. "We need to hurry, Arthur. Frederick Stanley and Inspector Farr need to show you something."

"The roses—" Arthur started, but Duke Ian replied, "Because you're the winner, all your roses will be placed in our greenhouse for more visitors to admire. You don't need to worry about them. They will be taken care of."

They walked to the carriages. Inspector Farr and Frederick Stanley followed them.

When Arthur saw an elderly servant standing next to a carriage, he slowed down. "I know him." And then he ran forward, calling, "Ham! Ham! It's me, Arthur!"

The elderly servant glanced at him, and then his knees buckled. "Arthur!"

Arthur put his hands around him and hugged him. "Ham, I recognized you immediately when I saw you."

Ham pushed Arthur further and studied his face and his posture. "You've grown up to be a fine young gentleman, Arthur."

"I'm no gentleman," Arthur replied.

Ham glimpsed curiously at Count Stanley, who approached them smiling; his eyes had tears in them. "Hammersmith, it looks like our boy recognized you first." Then he turned to Inspector Farr and Duke Ian, explaining, "Arthur was the only one who ever called Hammersmith Ham. He was too young to call him by his full name, so he always called him Ham."

"Another proof that Arthur is who we thought he was," the inspector replied.

"Who am I?" Arthur asked as he listened to the conversation standing next to Hammersmith.

Hammersmith turned to him and asked, "Don't you recognize Count Stanley? Look closely."

Arthur turned his eyes to Count Stanley. He studied the man's face. There was something familiar in the shape of it, the eyebrows, the hair color, the eyebrows... "Do I know you from somewhere, sir?" Arthur asked.

Tears filled Count Stanley's eyes as he replied, "Yes, my dear boy." He wiped his eyes. "You're my son, Arthur Stanley." He opened his arms. Arthur took a few steps forward, and they hugged.

Inspector Farr explained to Arthur, "You were kidnapped from your home when you were a young child. The kidnappers asked for ransom. However, another boy was hurt before the kidnappers contacted your parents with instructions on where to deliver the ransom. They never heard from them after that. They suspected you had died."

"I remember the basement and another boy who was scared and crying a lot. Darius was his name," Arthur said. "The men came in and dragged him away one day, and he kicked and cried that he wanted to see his mommy and go home."

"Yes, Darius was the other boy kidnapped about the same time as you," Inspector Farr replied. "He was blind when the kidnappers returned him home."

"Blind?" Arthur said, looking horrified. "He was a young, scared boy!"

"These kidnappers are ruthless. They don't care about anyone. My guess is you and Darius could recognize the kidnappers and identify them. That's why they had to blind him," Inspector Farr replied.

"That's possible," Arthur replied, and his brows drew together.

"You need to give me the description of the men you saw and any other detail of their voices, clothes, and what they said back then if you can remember. I know you were a small child, but sometimes the scary memories stick in your mind better than the good ones," Inspector Farr said seriously. "It's important that we capture these men. They have committed horrific crimes, and they need to be punished."

CHAPTER TWENTY-TWO

The Ride to Arthur's Old Home

The carriage ride took about twenty minutes to Count Stanley's stately estate. Inspector Farr had an official carriage with two policemen following the three other carriages. Count Stanley, Duke Ian Manchester, Arthur, and Inspector Farr rode in the first carriage, the ladies in the next one, Olivia Ackley's carriage was next, and the last one was the police officers. Inspector Farr had considered that because it was still an open criminal case, it was better to take with them the police officers in case Arthur's return would bring out the kidnappers.

During the ride, Inspector Farr kept asking Arthur for more details about the basement, the men he had seen taking Darius away, and then details of his escape.

Arthur closed his eyes to recall the past events. "I was kept in a dark basement for a long time," Arthur replied, frowning. "There was a musty smell like in an underground place, and I thought I heard some waves on the other side of the outer wall. The men throw in a pile of straws to lay on and two blankets, one for me and one for Darius. It was still cold, so we huddled together. At night, the rats came by and tried to bite me. Darius and I stayed awake one at a time to shoo away the hungry rodents. Sometimes we were too tired, and we both fell asleep, and then the rats came and bit us."

Inspector Farr made some notes in his notebook and mumbled, "Good, very good." Then looked up and said, "Describe the men who took you."

"It was not a man who took me. It was the servant girl who was with me outside that day," Arthur replied. "She said it was going to be a game, and we had to run to a carriage waiting for us by the road. So, I followed her. A man was waiting for us there, and he grabbed me and lifted me inside the carriage, where a woman took me. And then they drove away."

"The servant girl!" Count Stanley mumbled, and his hands tightened to fists. "She was part of the kidnapping plot! We never suspected her. She cried and said someone had hit her behind, but she didn't see anything. That liar!"

"We'll get her now," Inspector Farr replied. "We can track her down and punish her."

"She is still working at our estate but as a chambermaid," Stanley replied in a furious voice.

"The kidnappers wanted someone in your home in case Arthur ever returned," Inspector Farr replied. "We need to make sure we capture her before she can send a word to her partners in crime."

"Yes, it's better not to let her see Arthur," Duke Ian said. "We must get all the gang members before Arthur is safe."

"What can you tell me about the men in the basement?" Inspector Farr continued.

"The men who kept me in the basement were not neat. They looked like hard labor workers with unshaved faces and stained and patched clothes. One of them was called Simon. I think he was the boss."

"Excellent," Inspector Farr replied. "We've got more clues from you than we had before."

"How long were you there in that basement?" Inspector Farr asked.

"I think I was there the whole time after my kidnapping. The carriage that took me away stopped in front of a building by the River Thames, and the man in the carriage dragged me inside the building and down to the basement. That's how I knew how to escape when the right time came. "

Inspector Farr nodded and asked, "Can you describe the building where you were taken?"

"It was a grey stone building. The door had a crest on it. When the carriage rolled up to the house, I only saw it when I was dragged inside. I remember the river because I heard and smelled it."

"A crest?" Both Duke Ian and Inspector Farr leaned closer to Arthur.

"Yes, it was a bird with wings wide open," Arthur replied.

"I know that crest," Duke Ian said to Inspector Farr. "It's the House of Bassertons."

"Interesting." Inspector Farr scribbled down some notes and added, "It's one of the eldest noble families in London."

"And their income has always been a source of gossip. The ransoms might explain the sudden flux of money from time to time," Duke Ian replied.

"What did the woman look like?" Inspector Farr asked, turning to Arthur. He leaned on his knees and hung his head as he tried to recall the woman in the carriage.

"She wore a dark red colored dress and a wide-brimmed hat with black lace over her face. Her hair was dark brown, and she had a huge, red-stoned ring on her left hand. That's all I remember of her," Arthur replied and added, "And her voice, of course, was low and raspy, not like any woman's voice I've ever heard before."

"You have a very good memory, Arthur." Inspector Farr replied. "We will catch the gang, and based on your description, we now know the leaders of the kidnappers too: The Bassertons!"

"I'd be pleased to see them captured if they harmed Darius," Arthur said, and his eyes flashed with anger. "He was just a scared little boy."

"Tell me again how you escaped?" Inspector asked, turning his sharp eyes on Arthur.

Arthur nodded, leaned back on the seat again, and recalled the last evening in the basement. "It was right after they took Darius. I heard angry voices outside the door, and the man who usually brought food and water forgot to lock the door. He pulled it close like usual, but it didn't click, so I went to the door and pushed it open. I snuck upstairs and heard arguing voices in one of the rooms upstairs, but I didn't stay. I ran to the front door and snuck out. I'm sure no one saw me leaving because they were all in that one room fighting. I ran away as fast as possible, and then I found a park, stayed overnight, and slept on the bench. Then I met a group of orphan boys, and they let me join them. They helped me adjust to living as a street kid and find food and shelter. That was all before I met Duke Ian," Arthur explained, turned his eyes to the duke, and added, "I'm grateful that you took me to your country estate. I would have been in danger if I had stayed in London. The kidnappers would have found me eventually."

Duke Ian smiled brightly. "It was my pleasure. You saved my wife's and her father's life. You were always a smart kid. Now I know why," he said and turned his eyes to Count Stanton. "You have an intelligent son. He has received a good basic education at my house, and with some more studies, he will be a worthy heir for you."

Count Stanton beamed and replied, "I've noticed he is a smart boy." He looked at Arthur and asked, "Do you remember your mother and your home?"

"Some of it." Arthur closed his eyes, "I always thought it was just a dream. I remember a beautiful woman with blond hair singing to me and laughing happily. She had red and green jewels on her neck. I recall a big white building with stables. I had a pony I rode every day. The house had large rooms with beautiful shiny chandeliers and a room with lots of toys."

"That was my wife. She'll be excited to see you. And yes, you had started to learn how to ride with a pony," Count Stanton replied. Sighing, he added, "Your mother and I had a daughter after you went missing. Her name is Sarah. You've never met her."

Arthur's heart skipped a beat. "I have a little sister." He had always wished to have a real family. Now he had a father, a mother, and a sister. It all seemed like a dream.

"Yes, she is sixteen now. A beautiful young woman. We kept an eye on her and added security on the estate because we didn't want to lose another child."

"You did right. Now we know that one of your maids is part of the kidnapping plot," Inspector Farr commented.

Count Stanley glanced outside as the carriage turned to a side road that led to his estate. "We're home soon."

Arthur leaned to watch the views outside, but Inspector Farr pulled him back. "We need to keep you out of sight until we catch the maid."

Arthur nodded. "I understand. I didn't realize she might be watching the carriage too. I'll be more careful."

Count Stanley patted his knee and said, "It will only be a short moment until Inspector Farr takes that woman away, then you'll be free to look around."

CHAPTER TWENTY-THREE

The Maid

As soon as all the carriages were stopped in front of a large stately estate, Inspector Farr stepped outside to confront the two policemen he had asked to come with them. "We need to capture a maid. She's part of a kidnapping gang. Count Stanley will show us who she is."

Duke Ian went to the other carriage and told the ladies to wait for a moment before they got out. "Let the police do their work first, and then we'll explain everything." He then walked to Lady Olivia's carriage and explained the same thing. "I can go sit with Aislinn and Rose," Lady Olivia said. Duke Ian helped her to step outside. They walked back to the ladies' carriage, and she climbed inside. Ian returned to the first carriage to keep Arthur company.

Count Stanley followed Hammersmith inside. "Hammersmith, please find Adele. We need to talk to her," he said. Hammersmith nodded. He understood perfectly Adele was the one who had been with Arthur the day he disappeared. "Bring her into the library. We'll wait there."

When Hammersmith went to look for the maid, Count Stanley gestured for Inspector Farr and the policemen to follow him to the library.

In a couple of minutes, Adele came in with Hammersmith. When she saw the policemen, she paled. "What is going on, sir?"

"Miss, you are under arrest for kidnapping and torture and other crimes," Inspector Farr said, gesturing to the two policemen who went to stand next to Adele and handcuffed her.

"You now have a chance to speak up and give us your conspirators' names. It might help you in your sentencing," Inspector Farr replied.

"What? I haven't done anything," the maid replied, but her eyes shifted from side to side as if looking for a way to escape.

"If you wish to stay silent, you will be sentenced with your collaborators," Inspector Farr repeated. "This is your last chance to come clean."

Adele looked around and saw only serious faces. She sighed, and her shoulders slumped. "I guess it was coming. I knew that sooner or later, I was going to be caught." She paused, then added, "I helped to kidnap your young son years ago. I don't know how you found out about it. And none of the others were my collaborators. I only had a tiny part in the kidnapping. I was supposed to take the boy to the road where the carriage was waiting for him. That's all. They paid me a pound to do that."

"Give us the names of the persons who hired you." Inspector Farr stood in front of Adele and stared at her icily.

"The Bassertons. They were the leaders! The other men were just hired like I was. I only know Simon Salton and Marty Haggard by names." The maid looked down, and tears fell on her cheeks. "I never wanted anything to happen to the boy. He was a gentle and lovely kid."

"Take her away. I'll come with you, and we can go back to London now and get a team ready to arrest the rest of the kidnappers. I have great news for Superintendent Allender. He will be pleased to hear that we have the names of the leaders," Inspector Farr ordered his policemen, who grabbed the maid by the arms and walked her out. He turned, extended his hand to Count Stanley, and said, "I will return with them to London. I have lots of work to do."

Count Stanley replied, "Thank you. I'm sure we will meet again because Arthur will have to testify against the group in trial."

"Yes, you're right," Inspector Farr replied. "With the maid's confession, we have enough to charge the Bassertons and the other members. If they confess, too, it might not be necessary for Arthur to go to court. We'll see what happens."

When the maid walked out of the mansion escorted by the police, Ian climbed out of the carriage. "That's the guilty maid. Now we can go inside."

Arthur took a deep breath. He stepped outside and glanced around. The building was white like he remembered. He followed Ian to meet the ladies and smiled when Rose stepped outside. "Rose, this is my home." Then Arthur quickly explained everything.

"Then you can marry me!" Rose said, putting her arms around his neck and raising her happy face. Arthur grabbed her tight and kissed her fiercely.

Aislinn exhaled rapidly. "Rose! That's not how ladies act!"

Duke Ian laughed. "I guess we'll have a wedding soon."

Arthur kept Rose in his arms when he said, "I will marry Rose. I wanted to marry her when I was a servant. I'm not going to let her go. I love her."

"And I love Arthur," Rose added, keeping her hand in Arthur's.

"I know. I saw how you both looked at each other," Duke Ian replied. "Let's go inside. Arthur, your parents are waiting for you."

Meanwhile, Lady Victoria Stanley had joined her husband in the library with their daughter.

Arthur stopped by the doorway. They all stood still for a short moment, then Lady Victoria rushed to hug him. "Arthur! You're alive!"

Arthur's sister stared at him, puzzled. "Is this my brother who was kidnapped?" she asked her father, who nodded, smiling. "Yes, he is. He's home now."

CHAPTER TWENTY-FOUR

The Basserton's Residence

When Inspector Farr had returned to Scotland Yard, he arranged for the uniformed police officers to come with him in two carriages. Superintendent Allender came outside to greet Inspector Farr. "I'll see you when you get back. Good luck!"

Superintendent Allender was a young man but overworked. His eyes were set deep, and he looked tired. His suit was dark grey with a white shirt and vest under it. Capturing the kidnapper gang who had worked in London and among the wealthiest families would be excellent news, worth a promotion for both him and Farr, he thought. And if not a promotion, then perhaps more funds and more investigators, at least, he hoped.

As soon as the carriages stopped in front of a large stately estate, Inspector Farr stepped outside and went to the front door. His crew of police officers followed him and waited on the path leading to the house. Inspector Farr instructed them: "Get two men on the back, and make sure no one escapes." The police officers nodded, and two walked rapidly around the house to the backside.

While waiting for someone to open the door, Inspector Farr noticed the golden crest on the door: a phoenix with wings open. *That's the bird Arthur recalled. This is the house where he was taken after he was kidnapped*, he thought.

Inspector Farr rang the bell and confronted the butler who came to open the door and said with his most official commanding voice: "We are here on official business concerning some criminal activities conducted or led by the residents of this household. Please, let the owners of the house know and come to see me immediately."

The butler nodded, not even surprised, and gestured to a room on the other side of the hallway. "Could you all please wait at the salon? I will let Madam and her son know that you are here."

As Inspector Farr passed through the hallway and entered the salon, he took a deep breath, trying to calm himself and determine what sort of people these Bassertons were. *Snobby, of course,* he thought. *They would look down on him because he was not a nobleman. Duke Ian and Count Stanley were different. They appreciate hard-workers and intelligence of any man regardless of societal status.*

He stood by the French doors and viewed the rose bushes outside, noticing his two uniformed officers waiting in the garden for possible runaways.

The sun was setting, and it was getting late in the evening. The day had gone by fast because of the activities at the flower exhibition and then at Stanley's estate. However, it had been worth it because he had gotten a confession from the maid confirming Arthur's recollection of the kidnapping events years ago. That would be enough to arrest the Bassertons and send them to trial.

Inspector Farr heard a commotion in the hallway and turned around to see an agitated young man with an elderly woman marching into the saloon. "What is this outrageous intrusion into our privacy?" Lady Basserton demanded, waving a black cane with a golden eagle handle in her hand. She wore a dusty-rose-colored dress with a black lace shawl on her shoulders. Heavy golden ruby earrings hung from her ears, and she had a matching choker on her neck. Lady Basserton and her son both sported dark mahogany hair and similar facial structures: hawk nose, small sharp eyes, and narrow faces with high cheekbones. Inspector Farr thought they reminded him of caught wild animals growling and showing their teeth.

The young man said, "I'm Lord Basserton, and this is my mother, Lady Busselton. May I inquire what your unexpected business here is?" He didn't ask Inspector Farr to sit down or offer him anything to drink. They all stood in the room facing each other angrily.

Inspector Farr placed his arms behind his back and said calmly, "I'm here to arrest both of you and any coconspirators you have currently in this house. I also have a warrant to search the premises for any stolen goods and items acquired from crimes."

Lady Basserton took a deep breath, opened her mouth, and said, "This is... This is unbelievable! Do you know who we are?"

"Yes, I do know. We have gathered evidence to arrest you and your gang of kidnappers. Please, follow my officers to the carriages outside." Inspector Farr looked pleased as the uniformed officers grabbed Lady Basserton and her son and walked them outside to the waiting carriages. The rest of the police officers were ready to search the house.

When Lord Basserton heard Inspector's words, he looked deflated. His shoulders slumped. He knew their crime spree was done. There was nothing he could say or do to avert this arrest. He stood frozen, transfixed. He just stood there, unmoving, when the police officers pulled him by the arms to go with them.

Lady Basserton fought and cried, "Get your dirty hands off! I'm Lady Basserton. You can't do this to me. I will contact your superiors! This is disgraceful!" She struggled and tried to pull her arms free from the tight grip of the police officers but to no avail. She was walked outside after her son and was placed in a carriage with the uniformed officers. The carriage left the residence and headed back to Scotland Yard, where the two arrested criminals were put in cells to wait for the prosecution.

The police officers arrested all the household members present at the residence. Their stories would either set them free or put them in jail with the Bassertons. They found three rough-looking men in the stables and arrested them too.

It took over three hours for Inspector Farr and the officers to go through the building. They found the basement where the boys were kept. It still had some old moldy straws on the stone floor. It looked exactly like Arthur had described. Inspector Farr and one of the police officers glanced around. The officer had a lit candle with him to show the light. Inspector Farr noticed something glinting in the far corner of the cell. He went there and picked it up. A button with a flower on it. *This proves that Arthur was here*, he thought.

"Shine some more light on the corner over there," Farr asked the officer who followed the order. Inspector kicked away some straw and found a couple of pieces of fabric. *They could be part of clothes*, Farr thought. "Let's take these with us. They might belong to one of the kidnapped children," he said. They found a buckle of a child's shoe, which they also pocketed to bring with them.

They moved forward to the second floor and went through each bedroom. They found plenty of jewels and cash, which was not surprising if the owners of the house had requested the ransom to be paid in jewels, gold, or cash. They packed all of it with them, left the residence, and returned to Scotland Yard.

It was already night when their carriages turned to the front of the New Scotland Yard building on the Thames embankment. The River Thames looked dark like velvet as they passed it. Inspector Farr inhaled the smell of the river, a stench you'd never forget. Human excrement made it impossible to swim in, and it was unbearable to breathe on hot days. He quickly walked inside the building and smelled the familiar tobacco in the hallways as he headed to see his superior, Superintendent Allender. He knocked on Allender's door and immediately heard the response, "Come in."

Inspector Farr opened the wooden door and closed it behind him. He had the items gathered from the Bassertons with him, set them on the table in front of Allender, then sat down on a leather chair on the opposite side.

Farr said, "The Bassertons have been arrested. They are already in their cells waiting for the prosecution."

Superintendent Allender looked pleased. He took the button in his hand, and Farr said, "That's Stanley's crest. It proves Arthur was held in the basement."

They both looked at the pieces of cloth Farr had found in the basement and Allender asked, "Could these belong to the victims?"

"I assume so," Farr replied. "We need to study them at our laboratory and find out the material. It would give us more clues about what we are looking for." Then he pointed at the shoe buckle. "That is expensive. I bet it belongs to one of the kidnapped children kept in the basement."

"Go through the images of the kidnapped children. Perhaps, we get lucky and find out who wore shoes like that," Allender replied. He crossed his fingers on the table and said, "Great work, Farr. This will go into history. We have cracked wide open the biggest kidnapping case in London's history in decades."

Farr grinned. "It sure will. I'm grateful that we captured these criminals. They didn't care about the young children and only wanted money." He looked furious as he added, "What they did to that poor child, Darius, was despicable. Blinding a young child and driving him insane was cruel and unusual."

Superintendent Allender nodded. He took his cigarettes out of the drawer and offered one to Farr, who accepted it. "It's time to get our case together for the prosecutor. We have the masterminds now, but I don't know if we have all the gang members yet. We need to interrogate the Bassertons and their staff to see who will crack and give us more names. We also need to confiscate all their assets, so they can't buy their way out of this."

Farr replied, "Yes, the Bassertons will get the best solicitor to defend them. I'm sure of it. We need to have an airtight case before this goes in front of the judge."

"Contact that young fellow, Arthur, tomorrow, and ask him to come and see the buckle and the clothes. Perhaps, he can identify them," Superintendent Allender ordered, and Farr nodded.

He stood up and said, "I'll leave now to get a couple of hours of sleep."

"Good. You deserve it," Superintendent Allender said, then added, "I'll call and report to the top floor now. They need to know that the

Bassertons have been arrested for a series of kidnapping cases and that this case will be in the news soon."

"Yes, the Bassertons have powerful friends, but we'll see if any of them will be on their side when this case is out in the open and in court." Farr opened the door and said, "Good night."

CHAPTER TWENTY-FIVE

Duke Ian and Inspector Farr

Inspector Farr got up early and went to see Duke Ian Manchester. When he got there, Mattson opened the door. "Good morning, Inspector Farr. The duke is having breakfast. I'll show you the way."

Farr followed Mattson to a dining room where Duke Ian was sitting and having a strip of bacon, eggs, and toast with jam. He glanced up and smiled. "Good morning. You are early, Inspector. Would you like to have some breakfast too?"

"Good morning, Duke, and yes, I'd love to." Inspector Farr sat down, and a maid brought him a plate with eggs, bacon, and toast and placed a jam jar in front of him. Mattson brought orange juice and coffee to the table and served it to both men.

"So, how is the case going?" Duke Ian asked.

"Well, I think..." Farr paused his eating, looked at the duke, and added, "I hoped to find Arthur here. I need to get him to Scotland Yard. We arrested the Bassertons last night and then searched their house. We found some items and we'd like Arthur to look at them."

"He's staying with Stanleys for tonight. The family had gone through so much that I decided to leave the boy to stay there. They had lots to catch up on. I'll send a message for Arthur, and we can meet him at Scotland Yard." He gestured to Mattson and said, "Send a message to Stanleys and ask Arthur to meet us at Scotland Yard in a couple of hours." He glanced at Inspector Farr and asked, "Is that okay?"

Inspector Farr nodded. "Yes, that will be fine."

Mattson left and returned soon. He had given the orders to one of the servants.

While they finished breakfast, Inspector Farr told the duke the details of what they had found in the basement and mentioned the cash, gold, and jewelry they had gathered with them.

"I might be able to help with the jewelry. If there are any family heirlooms, I might recognize some of them. Also, you should contact Darius Fitzgerald's parents. They need to know that the kidnappers have been arrested. They might identify some jewelry, too," Duke Ian replied. He gestured to Mattson again. "Can you send a message to Lord Fitzgerald and ask if he would like to meet us at Scotland Yard? Mention that we have arrested his son's kidnappers."

Mattson nodded and went to take care of the order, then returned to the dining room after giving the message to one of the servants. *Busy morning,* he thought. He was also curious to know what the inspector had found at the Bassertons' residence.

"The shoe buckle looks expensive. I will show it to you to see if you can identify it, or perhaps Arthur can," Inspector Farr said while sipping his coffee. He took a biscuit, too, and bit it. *This is probably the best breakfast I've enjoyed all week*, he thought.

"Yes, the children had fancy shoe buckles back then. I'm sure it belonged to one of them," Duke Ian said with a distressed timber in his voice. He shook his head and added, "I can't believe that family. They tortured other families for money!"

"Yes, it is unbelievable. We have to make an air-tight case to ensure the Bassertons never do this to other families," the inspector replied fiercely.

"Arthur will help you. He lost his family for years and was lucky to find them again. Not all the children were as fortunate as he was. He stayed healthy, and he was taken care of," Duke Ian said.

CHAPTER TWENTY-SIX

At Scotland Yard

W hen Duke Ian and Inspector Farr entered the halls of the Scotland Yard, Arthur was already waiting for them there, pacing restlessly in the hallway, and his father, Count Stanley, had accompanied him there.

Duke Ian recognized Darius Fitzgerald's father in the hallway and greeted him first, introducing himself and Inspector Farr. "Good morning, Lord Fitzgerald. I don't know if you remember me, but I'm Duke Ian Manchester." He gestured to the inspector and introduced him. "This is Inspector Farr, who is investigating the kidnappings. He arrested the leaders of the kidnapping gang yesterday."

"Oh my!" Lord Fitzgerald sighed. "Yes, I do remember you. We've been at the House together."

Duke Ian nodded to Stanley and Arthur and added, "Then you must recognize Frederick Stanley, Count of Warrendale, and this is his son, Arthur." They all shook hands.

Lord Fitzgerald asked, "I thought your son was also kidnapped years ago."

"Yes, he was, but he came back recently. He is going to help to close this kidnapping case," Stanley replied.

Lord Fitzgerald looked like a man who had suffered a great loss in his life. His hair had greyed early, and his eyes were sad when he looked at Arthur. "I wish my son had returned healthy as you did."

"I knew your son, Darius. We were kept together in the basement. We slept together there for many nights before they took him away," Arthur replied. "He was my friend."

Lord Fitzgerald's eyes flickered in interest. "Perhaps, you'd like to come and meet Darius? He has not been doing so well since he was returned tortured. You know the criminals took away his eyesight. He didn't recover from that horror well at all."

"I'd love to meet him," Arthur replied firmly.

"Let's go to the room over there. We have some items in custody which I'd like you all to look at," Inspector Farr said, taking the lead and heading to the large meeting room at the end of the hallway. His supervisor, Superintendent Allender, came out of his office when he heard multiple voices in the hallway and joined the group. This case was the biggest in the decade, so he wanted to hear all the news immediately.

The items were spread on the large wooden table in the middle of the meeting room.

Arthur's eyes fixed on the piece of blue cloth, so worn and dirty that the color was barely visible. "I think that's part of my jacket I wore back then. I used it as my pillow in the basement."

Lord Fitzgerald took the shoe buckle in his hand and twirled it around. "This from Darius's shoe. He returned with only one buckle on his shoes." He turned to the inspector and added, "We kept all the clothes he wore when he was returned to us. You can have them and match the shoe buckle with the other one."

"Thank you, sir," Inspector Farr replied.

"These jewels. Some of them look old-fashioned. I believe I can recognize a couple of them," Duke Ian said and picked up a brooch with pearls and smaragds. "This one belongs to the family of Heddertons. I believe their daughter was kidnapped. They must have paid with jewels." He picked up a choker with a huge diamond in the middle. "This I've seen before. It belongs to Lady Anheim."

Inspector Farr wrote notes. He walked to the doorway and asked one of the investigators to bring all the kidnapping case files of the past two decades to the meeting room. It took several minutes before the investigator returned carrying a pile of case files.

"Stay here and help us go through these," Farr said, and the young man eagerly nodded. Being a part of this high-value case was a dream come true. Farr instructed, "Find the cases of Hedderton and Anheim in the files. We'll see what we can find in them." The young investigator nodded and started searching through the files. Soon, he found the two requested.

Inspector Farr walked to him, and they both looked over the case notes. "Yes, both had a child kidnapped, and they didn't have enough money to pay all the ransom in cash, so they gave some jewelry with it. That's good because now we have two more families that can testify against the kidnappers."

Some of the other jewelry was put aside for further examination.

They spent an hour in the meeting room going through the items. Then Lord Fitzgerald turned to Arthur and asked, "Would you like to come with me to meet Darius? I'd very much like him to see you."

Arthur nodded, and his father said, "I will come too. We can follow you with our carriage if that suits you?"

"Yes, perfectly fine. Thank you for coming with," Lord Fitzgerald said.

Duke Ian turned to Arthur and said, "Don't forget that Rose is expecting to see you tonight. She wants to hear all the details."

Arthur smiled and said, "I'll never forget my Rose. I will come by later tonight."

The Stanleys left after Lord Fitzgerald.

As they drove away in their carriages, Frederick Stanley said, "Arthur, do you know how sick Darius is? They have kept him in the mental hospital most of his life."

"I heard about his awful fate. Duke Ian told me." Arthur looked devastated. "I'm so sorry I couldn't escape with Darius before they took him away."

"It's not your fault, my son," Frederick Stanley replied and patted him on the knee. "You were just a child, and the kidnappers were ruthless people. They don't deserve to live in luxury the way they have. They need to be punished."

Arthur looked grim. "I will testify against the kidnappers if I'm asked. I don't mind telling everyone about my past. I hope that Rose doesn't either."

Frederick Stanley replied, "If she loves you like she seems to, then she won't care. She was ready to marry you when you were just a gardener, a servant at her father's estate."

Arthur nodded.

When Lord Fitzgerald's carriage turned to a small gravel path leading to a large brick building, Arthur straightened his back and viewed outside. *This is the sanitorium,* he thought.

As soon as the carriages stopped in front of the building, Arthur stepped outside and walked to the front door. He waited for his father and Lord Fitzgerald to catch up with him there. He was eager to see his old friend, although he was unsure what to expect. Darius was no longer a young, scared boy, but neither was he.

A nurse was sitting by the front counter when the three of them walked inside. She recognized Lord Fitzgerald immediately and came to greet him. "Good afternoon. Are you here to see Darius?"

"Yes, and these are my friends," Lord Fitzgerald replied. "How is my son?"

"Darius is having one of his good days." The nurse walked ahead, opened a door on the left side of the hallway, let them all inside, and closed the door behind them.

A young man was sitting by the window. He wore a dark blue morning robe and pajamas under it. When he heard the door opening and closing, he asked with a faint voice, "Is that you, Nurse Marshall?"

"No, my son. It's your father," Lord Fitzgerald replied gently. He went to his son and touched him on his shoulder. "I have two other men with me." He gestured for Arthur to come forward.

"Hello, Darius," Arthur said quietly.

Darius stiffened. "Who is that?" He had a dark cloth over his blinded eyes.

"It is me, Arthur, your old friend." Arthur saw Darius's hands tighten their grip on the armrests of his chair.

"Arthur?"

"Yes, it's me. Do you remember me? We were together in the basement," Arthur said. He was not sure if the memories of the basement were troublesome for Darius, but he decided to mention it anyway.

Darius held out his hand. It was shaking a bit. "Arthur? You got out! You're alive."

Arthur took Darius's hand and squeezed it tight. "Yes, we both got out."

"Please, tell me everything," Darius asked. Arthur pulled a chair closer to him and sat down. Then he told his life story, starting from the basement and when he ran out. And while he spoke, he held Darius's hand. They were together on this journey.

"I have news for you. The police arrested the kidnappers. They will be charged for what they did to you and all the other kidnapped children," Lord Fitzgerald said.

He had sat down with Frederick Stanley and watched the boys together.

"I can come home now," Darius said. "I'm ready. I don't have to be afraid of them after this," he added.

"Are you sure, my son?" Lord Fitzgerald asked, surprised.

"Yes, if Arthur can face them, then I will too. He will help me to face them," Darius replied. "They can't hurt me after this. No more nightmares."

"Let me inform the staff and talk to your doctor, and we'll see what they say," Lord Fitzgerald said and stood up.

Darius shook his head. "No, they will tell you that I need to stay here because they want you to keep paying them. I've been ready to leave this place for years. I was too depressed to demand any change, but now Arthur brought me new hope and faith that I can survive in the outside world. I'm ready."

Darius stood up and took his cane from the side of the chair. "I'm blind, but I'm not stupid. I can manage."

"Let me get your clothes," Arthur said and went to the closet and picked out Darius's day clothes: a white shirt, a blue jacket, and pants. He helped Darius get dressed and then picked a pair of boots from the wardrobe. Darius pulled them on himself. He was dressed to leave.

"I guess we'll go now," Lord Fitzgerald said. He was still stunned by the change in his son. He had always believed the doctors and nurses in this facility. He had never thought that his son was only depressed, not insane and that Arthur's visit was what he needed to stand up and leave the facility.

"It will be different and difficult for you to get used to the outside world," Lord Fitzgerald reminded his son.

"I know. I'll have to get used to it," Darius replied, giving him a rare smile.

It was the first time he had smiled in years.

Lord Fitzgerald took a deep breath and sighed. "Very well. Let's go then." He opened the door, and the four of them walked out.

Chapter Twenty-Seven

The Happy Ending

Darius, Arthur, the Anheims, Heddertons, and Stanley's maid testified against the Bassertons in their trial, and with the evidence found at their estate, they were soon convicted and sent to jail for the rest of their lives. They had no real defense in their case, so the trial was short and brutal.

The items belonging to the victims' families were returned to their rightful owners, as well as the money paid in ransom. The Bassertons lost all their assets, and their house was sold to cover the trial expenses and pay back to the victims.

Since meeting Arthur, Darius had been getting better every day. He had a silk cloth over his eyes, but his posture was straight, and his voice was steady when he testified in the court. His father beamed in the audience when he saw his son brave and unwavering on the stand.

Arthur and Darius stayed friends. They helped each other to adjust to changes in their new lives. Arthur learned to act like a nobleman and not as a servant, whereas Darius needed help to adjust to the outside world and the crowds. They attended a couple of balls together. Darius was still a handsome-looking young man from a wealthy family, even if he was blind, and thus, a potential candidate for marriage.

Arthur got ready for his wedding ceremony with Rose. They were called London's most besotted couples. Everyone noticed how in love they were. Both Duke Ian and Aislinn were excited about the upcoming wedding, and the Stanleys were happy to see their families joined together because Duke Ian was the one who had saved their son from street life.

The families did not rush the wedding planning. Rose got her most adorable lacy dress. Regardless of the kiss Rose had given to Arthur at Stanley's estate, they didn't want to marry in a hurry.

The only question before the ceremony was: When would Arthur give her a ring?

Lord Stanley approached Arthur one morning in the greenhouse and said, "I would like you to give Rose one of our family's rings as a wedding ring if that suits you. I've waited so long to have my son back that it is incredible to have you standing there and continuing my research work with plants and flowers."

"I'd be honored to have one of the family rings to give to Rose," Arthur replied.

Lord Stanley put his hand in his pocket and pulled out one sapphire ring and one diamond ring. "This sapphire ring belonged to my mother, your grandmother. And this diamond ring was the one I used to engage your mother. Please, give them to Rose. She is a darling girl and so much in love with you."

"I will thank you, father," Arthur replied and pocketed the rings.

He gave one to Rose the same night and the other she got on their wedding day. The bride and groom were seen smiling and laughing at the wedding ceremony near Duke Ian's estate at the local church. Rose had requested the small church because their maid Lillian had married the pastor there, and she wanted to have a familiar face marry her. Lillian had also made her wedding dress: a lacy satin dress with a long trail. Arthur had picked out the roses for the bouquet: white and pink roses with tiny forget-me-nots. Rose looked like an angel when she walked down the aisle with Duke Ian. After the ceremony at the church was over, the party continued at Duke Ian's estate after the wedding.

Made in the USA
Monee, IL
23 February 2025

12797740R00075